Wildings

'It may be that badger-watchers,
in company with bird-watchers,
are not entirely human.'

EILEEN SOPER
When Badgers Wake.

Wildings

The Secret Garden of
EILEEN SOPER
Duff Hart-Davis

H. F. & G. WITHERBY LTD

By the same author

Ascension: the Story of a South Atlantic Island
Peter Fleming: a biography
Monarchs of the Glen
Fighter Pilot
Hitler's Games: the 1936 Olympics
Armada
Country Matters
The House the Berrys Built

Novels
The Megacull
The Gold of St Matthew
Spider in the Morning
The Heights of Rimring
Level Five
Fire Falcon
The Man-Eater of Jassapur
Horses of War

First published in Great Britain September 1991 by
H. F. & G. Witherby Ltd
14 Henrietta Street, London WC2E 8QJ
Second impression October 1991

Text © Duff Hart-Davis 1991
Illustrations © the Estate of Eileen A. Soper 1991
Illustrations by George Soper © The Estate of George Soper 1991

The painting of Eileen aged eight by her father is
reproduced by courtesy of Fine-Lines Fine Art
(L. W. & R. M. Guthrie), The Old Rectory at 31 Sheep Street,
Shipton on Stour, Warks CV36 4AE.

A CIP catalogue record for this book is available from
the British Library

ISBN 0 85493 209 7

Typeset, printed and bound in Great Britain by
Butler & Tanner Ltd, Frome, Somerset

Acknowledgements

I SHOULD LIKE to thank the following for their memories of Eileen:

Alison Boardman, Michael Clark, Graham Field, Colin Franklin, Malcolm and Hilda Holt, Mike Kendall, Jessie Kerr, Sir John Lister-Kaye, Bt, Nigel Longmore, Ernest G. Neal, Marguerite Roe and Ray Walker.

Above all, I am grateful to Robert Gillmor, whose enormous enthusiasm for the Sopers' art is matched by his generosity in giving time, help, informed advice and excellent picnic lunches to intruders trespassing on his own territory of wildlife painting.

DUFF HART-DAVIS
March 1991

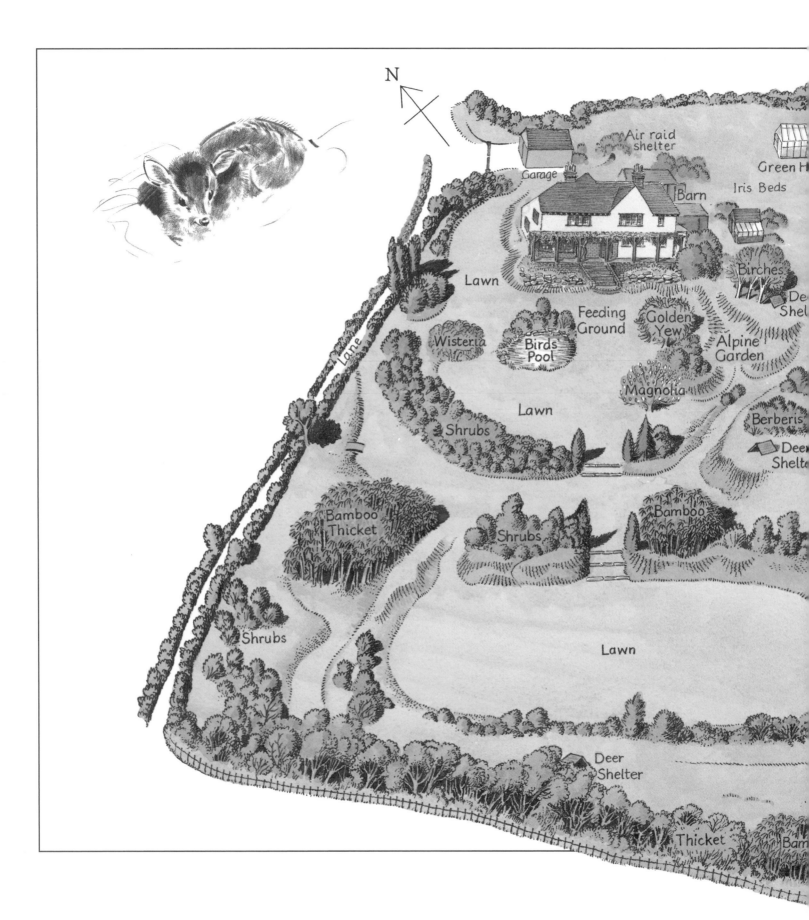

Wildings

THE GARDEN SANCTUARY

Spinney

Oak

Rose Garden

Iris | Iris

Laurels

Crab

Currant Bushes — Deer Shelter

Orchard

ls

Woodland

Wych Elms

Hazels

Bog

Water Garden

Scrub

Summer House

Rowans

Hawthorn Scrub

Thicket

Deer Shelter

Chalk Bank

Thicket

Robert Gillmor after Eileen A. Soper

Eileen Soper aged eight, painted by her father, 1913

One

ON THE NIGHT of 4 March 1989, three weeks short of her eighty-fourth birthday, the artist Eileen Soper fell ill at her home in Hertfordshire. Until then, although severely bent with arthritis, she had been in tolerable health, and her mind was still keen; but the sudden rupture of a blood-vessel in her leg demanded professional treatment, and in the morning she was taken into the Queen Elizabeth II hospital at Welwyn, a few miles away. Her sister Eva, four years older, was also taken into care, for although not seriously ill she had become enfeebled, both physically and mentally, and could not stay in the house on her own.

For most of her long life Eileen had harboured an unreasoning dread of hospitals – so much so that if ever she had to drive past one she made a detour to give it an even wider berth. To have landed suddenly in hospital was therefore the ultimate horror, and she was utterly miserable. A vegetarian, used only to the company of her sister, she hated the routines – and the food – of an institution. On 9 March she telephoned Longmores, her solicitors in Hertford, asking urgently for help; the call was answered by Graham Field, who in recent years had taken over her affairs. When he went to see her next morning she begged him to get them out: the food, she said, was killing them. Could they not go home? Medical considerations prevented their quick discharge, but later in March Field arranged for them to be moved to a nursing home.

Eileen was naturally anxious about their house, Wildings, at Harmer Green, and in April she asked Field to go over and look at it, to make sure that all was well, adding a request that he should not disturb the mice that were nesting in her slippers. With him he took Michael Clark, a long-term friend of Eileen's and a fellow-naturalist with a special interest in badgers, who lived close by.

Clark had often visited Wildings in years past, but Field had

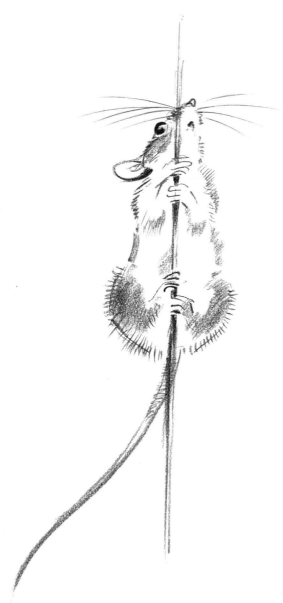

never seen the house, and now he was astonished by it. The four-acre garden, once the place's great glory, had gone wild and closed in on the building. Vegetation had advanced right to the grey, stuccoed walls and even on to the roof. A stout wooden trellis running the length of the south front was so smothered with wisteria and clematis that part of it had collapsed under the weight. Creepers had forced their way into the upper windows. At the back of the house a tree had fallen across the path and lay against the wall, half blocking the doorway. Ten-foot saplings sprouted from what had once been lawns. Roses, unpruned for years, had grown to a height of twelve or fifteen feet. Garden sheds were collapsing. Dead trees lay where they had toppled, and parts of the jungle were so thick that Field, trying to find the boundaries of the property, could barely fight his way through.

Inside the house, the scene was still more extraordinary. Rather as Howard Carter, peering through the first breach into the tomb of Tutankhamen, saw a dense mass of objects piled before his eyes, so the visitors to Wildings were confronted by an astonishing accumulation of possessions. Most of the rooms were full to the doorways, partly of furniture, but mainly of apple boxes, cardboard cartons, carrier bags and bundles of paper. Always a human squirrel, Eileen had rarely managed to throw anything away, and now her nest was crammed with the detritus of a lifetime's work. The former kiln-room, on the ground floor, was so stuffed with boxes that the visitors could penetrate no further than a couple of feet beyond the door: the kiln still stood in one corner, a large etching-press occupied the centre of the floor, and on top of a cupboard were piled brown paper parcels, not touched for years, containing eighteenth-century shop ledgers full of fine quality hand-made paper, which Eileen's father George Soper had used for his etchings.

The rest of the room was solid with cartons. Most of them contained papers: income-tax returns fifty years old, bank statements from the second world war, copies of ancient correspondence with book publishers, drafts of poems scribbled on the backs of torn-up cornflakes packets, share offers long obsolete, company reports and prospectuses – thousands upon thousands of sheets of paper, carelessly folded and crumpled, stuffed down tight upon each other in dense packs. But there were also old magazines and newspapers by the thousand, books stacked in piles on the floor,

rolls of material ordered but never used, pairs of shoes carefully packed inside plastic bags and then stowed inside other bags.

The high-ceilinged studio, on the first floor at the back, was also packed with books and papers, as well as with framed and unframed oil paintings by both Eileen and her father; another upstairs room contained box after box of empty jam jars, which turned out, when counted, to number over 3000. Mice were nesting not only in Eileen's slippers but also in the chest of drawers on the landing and in other comfortable resorts. From the stores in the kitchen it looked as though the sisters had lived exclusively on milk jellies and biscuits, but there were ample stocks of food for birds and other wild creatures. The whole house felt damp, and by normal standards it was thoroughly unkempt, for the tremendous volume of belongings had made cleaning impossible for many years.

Field's most immediate worry was the pictures. Apart from those stacked in the studio, many hung on the walls, and some were clearly of value. He needed expert advice, and when he asked Eileen for the name of someone who could give it she at once suggested the distinguished bird-artist Robert Gillmor, President of the Society of Wildlife Artists, with whom she had maintained contact for more than fifteen years.

Summoned from his home in Reading, Gillmor drove over to Hertfordshire, where he found Eileen beset by two main anxieties: one was that she and Eva should return to Wildings as soon as possible, the other that she should somehow arrange publication of an anthology of country writing on which she had been working for some time. Her idea was that the book should be illustrated with her father's wood engravings, and perhaps with his etchings as well, and that it should act as a memorial to him. Using two large folios for scrapbooks, she had pasted them up as dummies, sticking copies of the pictures between typewritten excerpts of prose and poetry; and Gillmor, who until then had not known much about George Soper's work, was immediately struck by the engravings – by their rich use of black and white, and by the way in which they retained the spontaneous freedom and fluidity of the artist's drawings.

In London he showed the scrapbooks to a publisher, David Burnett; but he, although enthusiastic about the engravings, felt that no book of that kind would sell unless illustrated in colour. Were any paintings available? The question sent Gillmor back to

Hertfordshire for a thorough search of the studio. On his first visit to Wildings he had been astonished by the decrepitude of the house, and by the amount of bric-à-brac it contained. Yet now a still greater surprise lay in store: among all the junk in the studio, stuffed into drawers, piled up behind pieces of furniture, was hidden an immense treasure trove of artwork, which he slowly brought to light; some of it was foxed by damp or nibbled at the edges by mice but most was in excellent condition and of exceptional quality. From the hand of George Soper there were 177 watercolours of horses working on the land, 71 wash-and-pencil drawings, 116 illustrations, 445 landscapes and 53 unfinished works, besides 3500 prints and a large number of sketchbooks – none of them seen by any outsider since the death of the artist in 1942. His daughter had left an equally rich harvest: apart from hundreds of prints made from early etchings, and an enormous number of drawings, there were more than 300 watercolours of the badgers, foxes, deer, stoats, squirrels, hedgehogs, otters, birds and other creatures to whose study she had devoted herself. Applying the most conservative judgement, Gillmor estimated the value of the unframed pictures in the studio at £900,000.

This book is the story of the strange, reclusive woman who allowed that hoard to accumulate, and of how she lived and worked in the heart of her secret garden: Eileen Alice Soper.

Two

Ada Lehany, George Soper's bride

S HE WAS BORN on 26 March 1905 in a house known as Redda-ford, in East Barnet Road, Enfield, North London, the second daughter of George and Ada Soper, and on her birth certificate the occupation of her father was given as 'Artist, Black and White'; but when she was only three the family moved to a new house that George had just built out in the Hertfordshire countryside, and there she spent the remaining eighty-one years of her life. Two influences, above all others, shaped the course of her existence: one was the large wild garden that surrounded the new house, and the other was her father.

Although in later life Eileen scarcely mentioned her mother, who seems to have been a kind but passive character, she never ceased to extol the achievements of her father. Even on her deathbed she spoke proudly of his prowess as an artist, his professionalism, his skill as a gardener, his great love of the countryside, his feeling for country people; above all, she treasured his deep knowledge of working horses, and the sympathetic accuracy with which he depicted them in action. She also took pains to emphasise that she herself never went to art school, but was taught to draw, etch and paint entirely by him.

George Soper was a West Countryman. Born in Devon in 1870, the son of a gardener, he was brought up there and in Somerset; but at some stage he was sent away to boarding school at Rams-gate – and the survival of a single letter home gives a startling glimpse of the establishment's formality. 'My dear Parents,' he wrote, in a painfully precise copperplate hand, on 13 December 1883:

Mr Pygott wishes me to present his compliments, and to inform you that the Christmas Vacation will commence on Thursday, the 20th Instant, on which day I hope to reach the Holborn Viaduct Station at 10.58 . . .

My dear Parents,
Your loving Son,
George Soper.

As a young man he entered the Royal Navy, but seems later to have transferred his allegiance to the army, for in 1893 he enlisted in the 20th Middlesex Artists Rifle Volunteers. In matters of art, he was largely self-taught, but he studied etching for a while under the leading practitioner of the craft, Sir Frank Short, at the South Kensington School of Art. He first exhibited at the Royal Academy in 1889, when he was only nineteen, and he continued to have pictures hung there almost every year for the rest of his life – a record of remarkable consistency. He was an exceptionally versatile artist, able to turn his hand to many kinds of work, but with a particular gift for drawing the human figure in action; and this talent he put to good use as an illustrator, especially in war scenes. At the turn of the century he poured out enormous numbers of highly animated illustrations for books, book jackets, magazines and journals: many depicted exciting episodes of empire building or defence, with colonial types under attack by spear-wielding natives whom the artist would probably have described as fuzzy-wuzzies. Among the classics he illustrated were *Alice's Adventures in Wonderland*, Kingsley's *The Water Babies*, Lambs' *Tales from Shakespeare* and Grimm's *Fairy Tales*. He made several trips to the Continent, at least one of them a journey to Switzerland, to illustrate Reginald Farrer's *Among the Hills*.

At heart George Soper was a countryman: a shy man, not drawn to the bright lights of society like his contemporary Alfred Munnings, but more at home in fields and woods, on the open Downs of Sussex or the Norfolk marshes. As he grew older, his principal subject became the land, and the men and horses who worked it. He spent countless hours in observation and sketching, but he did not merely watch teams at work, ploughing, harrowing, reaping or extracting timber from the woods: he also talked endlessly to the horse-handlers, walked up and down beside them and shared their hard, monotonous toil, with the result that he became able to express every facet of their existence with remarkable fidelity. As Eileen herself recalled, 'He was out on the harvest field,

George Soper as a young man

in the lane with the timber team, or with the men at "beaver" [break], seeking under a hedge some shelter from the biting wind. He shared the dust of the threshing machine and the bitterness of winter, following the mangold cart beside cattle in the snow – always with sketchbook in hand.' One contemporary commentator – the leading authority on prints, Malcolm C. Salaman – wrote lyrically of how his dry-point etching 'Timber-Hauling, Devon' captured the 'very stress in the movement of those two horses, the weight behind them in the huge log they have to haul. What vigour of muscle they are putting into the effort; how their knees bend to it, how their hooves dig into the ground!'

Yet Soper was by no means a yokel. The refinement of his art was matched by a certain fastidiousness in matters of dress and appearance. He was only about 5′ 6″ tall, and photographs show him to have been something of a dandy, always wearing high, starched white collars, tightly knotted ties or elaborate cravats, and stylishly cut tweed suits. Even if he dressed up specially for the camera – as people often did in those days – there is still a touch of flamboyance in the elegant sweep of his hair and the precise trim of his moustache.

By the 1890s he was living at 300 Amhurst Road, in North London, and when he began to pursue Miss Ada Lehany, daughter of a boot manufacturer, of 58 Clissold Road, Stoke Newington, not far from his own home, he pressed his suit by sending her letters in envelopes decorated with delicate little paintings – a snowscape, ivy leaves against the moon, daffodils. His courtship lasted for at least five years; and in the end, enchanted by his artistic chivalry, she accepted his proposal, and the couple were married in the parish church of Stoke Newington on 20 July 1897.

Ada was a fine-looking girl, with a long, elegant face and a determined jut to her chin that belied her gentle nature. A better clue to her character came from her eyes, which were deep-set and kindly. Evidently she was better off than her fiancé, for it was to her that tradesmen addressed their accounts for mattresses, pillows, a bolster, a dining table, chairs and various other pieces of furniture before the wedding. Their first child, Eva, was born in March 1901, and Eileen four years later. Both girls had conspicuously beautiful hair: Eva's was deep auburn or chestnut, with a natural wave in it, Eileen's straight and fine, like a cascade of radiant red-gold.

After Devon and Cornwall, George's favourite county was

Sussex, and he also worked in Somerset and Norfolk. By 1907, however, he had moved to Enfield, and through a friend he heard a plot of building land was available near the hamlet of Harmer Green, out in the wilds of Hertfordshire, due north of London. Ironically enough, the plot became available through one of the first in a long series of sales that destroyed huge areas of once-lovely countryside – a disastrous process, which Eileen herself never ceased to lament. By breaking up the High Welwyn estate, the auctioneers were able to offer 'thirty-three lots of exceedingly attractive building land … charmingly situated in the parishes of Welwyn and Digswell, Herts', commanding 'magnificent woodland views of great extent' and 'suitable for the erection of family residences and villas'. What partially saved the area for the time being was the fact that the plots were large – many of them extending to six acres or more – so that building did not seem too intense; but the process of suburbanisation had been irrevocably set in motion.

This did not worry George Soper. The sight of the plot – a one-acre strip of open field in the hills outside Welwyn, beside a lane which undulated and wound between overgrown banks and hedges – excited him greatly, for it offered exactly what he had been seeking: a site on which to create a large garden. In October 1907 he bought it – or, rather, Ada did, and the deeds were made

The house shortly after completion

out in her name. The house – described by its builders, Messrs Fairhead, as a cottage – went up during 1908. The Sopers paid the first instalment of £250 on 6 January, a second instalment of £200 on 15 February, and the final one of £75 on 23 April. A few last-minute adjustments made during the summer brought the total bill for the new house to £557–19–6.

A more prescient owner might have sited his dwelling deeper within his territory and further from the lane, for although traffic was light in those days, it has increased ever since. As it was, the house went up scarcely ten yards from the road. Legend has it that George himself planned the building, in collaboration with a local architect; if this is true it must be said that he was better at etching and painting than at designing houses, for this one turned out cramped and poorly planned. A medium-sized, oblong, two-storey structure, of undistinguished appearance, with white stuccoed walls, leaded windows and rather mean, low ceilings, it can never have been easy to run. The most direct way in from the lane led to an impossibly awkward back door which opened inwards into a tiny vestibule, making every entry and exit an act of a contortionist. Then came the kitchen, and, next to it, a narrow, stone-flagged parlour. Beyond that, from a cupboard-like hall inside the front door, an extremely steep staircase went up to the first floor, which had three bedrooms. At ground level, the only two rooms of any size were the sitting-room at the front and the studio, with a skylight in its sloping roof, at the back.

If the house's most important feature (for Soper) was the studio, its most attractive was the big, L-shaped window that ran right round one corner of the sitting-room, facing south and west, with only a slim iron pillar to support the corner of the building. Furnished with a broad bench-seat, the window commanded an excellent view of the land, and of the terrace, floored with brick, which ran the length of the building's south front. Above the terrace was built a trellis or pergola of heavy wooden beams, designed to support climbing plants such as wisteria, clematis and roses. Local memory relates that when Eileen went to live in the house, at the age of three-and-a-bit, she hated it – but the reason for her dislike is not known. Her father gave the place no name, heading his writing paper with the stamped legend GEORGE SOPER, HARMER GREEN, WELWYN, HERTS; not until after his death, many years later, did Eileen call the house 'Wildings'.

Apart from its proximity to the road, the site was well chosen, for the ground fell away invitingly in front of the terrace, and on a series of descending levels George set about planting an extensive, semi-wild garden. As Eileen herself described it,

> The garden was created on the slope of a meadow overlooking a wide landscape of field and woodland, open to the south wind, to sunlight and changing skies. Shaped to the artist's vision, it lost little of the wild element, and the meadow was never entirely tamed. But in time growing trees and shrubs changed its character.

Not only was George an enthusiastic and knowledgeable amateur botanist: he was also a conservationist, long before that term became fashionable, and his aim was to create a sanctuary in which birds and animals could live at peace. He never intended that the garden should be a formal one: rather, he wanted a luxuriant wilderness of interesting plants, with islands of cultivation among them, and clematis and wild roses scrambling over everything. His special interest was ferns, which he imported from many exotic sources and planted in huge clumps along his north-western border,

just inside the lane, until in the end he had more than ninety varieties growing there. Over the years further purchases of land gradually extended the original plot from one acre to four, and since the further reaches of it consisted of shrubbery and woodland it did indeed become a haven for many wild creatures. As Eileen's own plan of the garden shows, the only formal areas were those immediately in front of the house, round the two lawns (each on its own level), and the rose garden and iris borders to the east: the rest of the land provided ideal habitat for creatures great and small.

The garden was a nightmare for anyone trying to maintain order, since its steps and different levels meant that wheelbarrows were almost useless. For children, however, it made a thrilling playground: paths twisting in and out between tall clumps of fern and bamboo were like tracks through primeval jungle, and it is hardly surprising that the two girls, growing up in such natural surroundings, came to share their father's interest in plants and wildlife. By her own account Eileen was a bit of a tomboy, much given to climbing trees, particularly a willow that her father planted. For a while George kept bees, about which he used to tell an amusing story against himself. Once, when very young, Eileen was stung, and in an attempt to restore her confidence he led her, still in tears, to the hive, explaining that the bees would not molest her unless she annoyed them – whereupon one flew out and stung him smack on the nose.

To their neighbours, the Sopers seemed a happy and normal family – and a picture that George painted of Eileen when she was about eight confirms the impression of an idyllic childhood. There sits a cherubic, red-haired little girl, absorbed in a book, with a faithful teddy bear at her feet, and a ruddy glow from the red leather chairback imparts to the whole scene a sense of deep security. Yet George had one peculiarity which exercised a profound influence on the lives of both his daughters: an obsession with disease. Their nanny, Annie Harris, used to love taking them out in their pram, because every woman they met commented on the children's beauty, praised their glorious hair, and wanted to pet them; yet she often found herself in difficulty, for Mr Soper repeatedly forbade her to make contact with other people, in case the girls should catch some germ. She was not allowed to let anyone approach the children or touch them – and still less was she allowed to enter any strange house. Later, when Eileen was grown up and

Early days at Wildings

GREAT TIT *Parus major*
Rosa canina andersonii

21

Eva (left) and Eileen in the garden willow and (opposite) with their father, early 1920s

fell ill with appendicitis, her father's dread of hospitals was such that he insisted on her remaining at home, and got the gardener to scrub down a wooden table so that the surgeon could operate in the studio. In the early days such eccentricities no doubt seemed harmless enough, yet their long-term effect was incalculable; for as time went on the fear of disease in general developed into an unreasoning phobia about cancer, which powerfully reinforced the girls' natural shyness and encouraged them to shut themselves off from the rest of the world.

Eileen later suggested, without quite saying as much, that she was educated privately; but although it was certainly her father who taught her art, she did go to school for a while – first with Olive Downing, a tiny, gentle woman who ran a private school at her home in Knebworth, and then to Hitchin Girls' School, to which the sisters would travel by train from the station at Welwyn North, just down Harmer Green Lane. It is said that Eileen hated school, and perhaps this is why in later life she expunged it from her own record; perhaps, also, it was the excessive formality of her father's education that made him keen to keep his daughters at home.

To judge from the few documents that survive, Eileen's relationship with her parents was easy and cheerful. Within the family she was known as Pip, her mother as Blossom or Bloss. When the sisters went off on holiday, George sent them jaunty letters, beginning 'Dear Girls' and ending with his characteristic salutation, 'Cheer I O, everyone, Dad.' When he himself was on holiday, he wrote home in the same vein. 'Dear All & Girls,' he once began a letter from near Lewes. 'This place is A 1. The Downs all round. Had a walk over them this morning for nearly an hour before breaker, which is not served till 9. They bring a cup of tea up at 8 with the hot water. This morning Fred and I went off over the same ground and tried to do a rick-building subject. It was lovely in the sunlight – the Downs are much larger and more extensive than Amberley way, and there is more variety generally for

sketching. In fact we could not be in a better spot.'

When the girls went away, their mother sent loving, chatty messages, filled with whatever thoughts happened to pass through her mind as she was writing. 'Dear Evie and Eileen,' she scribbled when once they had gone to the south coast with Olive. 'Sorry the Major is late with the meals and so forgetful I should wake him up you are paying enough to get good attention. I hope he will buck up.' Then again, 'I think the Major is an old humbug, I guess you won't stay with him again in a hurry.' An occasional hint confirms that Eileen was a bit of a tomboy: 'I guess Eileen enjoyed trying to wake up the cops but I expect she was not quite wild enough in her escapades for them to make an excuse to nab her. What an awful shock it would have been to us old people to find you had all been had up by the police.' Ada's main preoccupation seems to have been that the girls were underweight. 'Be sure and have plenty of good food,' she wrote, 'or you will not get any heavier which will be a great pity as you are all much too thin.'

When the First World War broke out in 1914, George volunteered for military service at the age of forty-four, but was rejected on the grounds that he had a weak heart (in July 1918 an army medical board found him to be 'permanently and totally unfit for any form of Military Service', and discharged him from any liability to be called up). His contribution to the war effort was pictorial: working fast, and often late into the night, he illustrated partworks describing particular battles and the conflict in general, and hurried to London by train in the morning, taking his finished pictures with him.

Three

IN RETROSPECT, the most striking features of Eileen as a child are her precocity and her aptitude for work. As she herself wrote, from the moment at which she was old enough to hold a pencil her only desire was to follow in her father's footsteps, and she studied under him 'from a very early age'; she made her first etching when she was thirteen, and a year later George sent four of her prints to California, where they were hung at an exhibition in Los Angeles. In the spring of 1921 two of these – 'The Broken Gate' and 'The Swing', both measuring seven inches by five – were hung by the Royal Academy in London. Still only fifteen, Eileen became the Academy's youngest-ever exhibitor, and thereby caused a sensation. When the news broke that the artist was a mere girl, the judges came under fire – but critics received a robust riposte from Claude Shepperson, himself a well-known etcher and a member of the Academy's jury:

> We judge the work, not the persons. We do not know the painter's name, and it does not matter to us if the artist is three or three hundred . . . Looking at the work from an artistic standpoint, we had no hesitation in accepting it. It is no fault of ours that Miss Soper, aged fifteen, can hold her own with the giants of old days. We are proud of the girl, while of course sorry for the giants.

Suddenly Eileen was famous, not merely in England but in America, too: newspaper articles on both sides of the Atlantic described how she loved children, how she sought them out at play in Hertfordshire villages, how she captured their antics and emotions with rare spontaneity. In 1922, when she again exhibited at the Royal Academy, the London *Star* remarked that she 'should

Eileen with etching plate in the studio

have a brilliant career, if the records of other precocious exhibitors count for anything', and pointed out that artists who had had pictures hung at Burlington House when they were only sixteen included Millais and Landseer. Her prints were exhibited in Chicago, where the real-estate tycoon Wallace L. DeWolf, Chairman of the print committee of the Chicago Art Institute, became so fascinated by her that he presented the Institute with a collection of her work, first buying seven prints, then – in 1929 – another sixty-three. Critics praised the artist's rhythm, movement and sincerity, and also her restraint in not crowding her plates with superfluous detail.

Her etchings had an extraordinary effect on Americans. 'No matter how often a Genius comes before us, it is always a miracle in one form or another,' wrote one critic, Lilian Rea.

In the case of Eileen Soper, the personality and the work together make up the miracle. It is that of a child portraying children ... On all her plates these dream children come and go ... They appeal to the heart as well as to the eye, smooth out twisted nerves and revive one's earliest, most treasured memories, when the heart was young and life a dream of grown-up days that should be full of the delight of childhood.

An article by Patricia Talbot in the issue of the American magazine *Good Housekeeping* for July 1923, entitled 'A Schoolgirl among the Masters' and illustrated by five of Eileen's etchings, produced a flurry of fan-mail. 'The dear children are so alive and so cunning – I love them,' wrote Harriet Brakenridge from Berkeley, California. 'This note may never reach you, but if it does I would like you to know how much your work is admired and appreciated.' From British Columbia a bank manager besought her to illustrate his book *Peggy and her Playmates*, into which he had put 'prose and nonsense verse and serious verse and squirrels and blue jays, and gophers and beavers and butterflies. Illustrated by you, we would have the publishers on their knees. Carroll wrote *Alice in Wonderland*, but Tenniel made it.'

Nature and children 'are so beautiful together', Eileen replied; but, alas, she was far too busy to take up the offer, as she was 'continually turning down new work'. She wrote this letter in her own hand, but one senses that she was on a tight rein, and that her father was keeping close control over her output and her reputation. Thus when in 1923 the publishers Longman, Green wrote asking if she would do some drawings to illustrate *A Child's Garden of Verses*, by Robert Louis Stevenson, George answered that she could not accept the commission.

English critics also threw themselves into paroxysms of purple prose as they tried to describe the impact of the etchings. In a pamphlet entitled 'Some Thoughts on the Art of Eileen Soper' Haldane Macfall found it a miracle that she could depict real children, rather than the 'manikins, repulsive and ridiculous', of the Old Masters:

Eileen Soper has had the good fortune to escape the mimicry of the dead in art schools, and the even better fortune to possess as father an artist, and that artist an etcher ... She is wholly devoid of the mechanical stuff of the art schools; she addresses herself to utter the impression desired quite simply and with a purity of artistic intention thoroughly attuned to the years of innocence – as pure and passionless as, and akin to, the boy's voice that rises above the harmonies of the choir in the anthem's solo of some great cathedral, possessing a quality that the greatest opera singer can never know. It will be vastly interesting to see what the future will develop in the artistic utterance of this gifted girl when womanhood comes to her and the more complex observations of womanhood.

With her fame noised abroad by effusions of this kind, Eileen began to earn good money, selling prints on both sides of the Atlantic, and already she had in her the makings of an astute businesswoman. When the Royal Glasgow Institute of Fine Arts sold a copy of 'The Hurt Paw' for £2–12–6, but then discovered a discrepancy in the price, which she had raised, on her advice note, to £3–13–6, she was apologetic, but stood her ground. 'I am evidently in error', she wrote. 'The correct price should have been £3–13–6. This is rather unfortunate, as it is the last print. Would you kindly put it to the purchaser, and if he objects, the sale

'Flying Swings' was bought by Queen Mary in 1924.

Success brought fine motor cars to Harmer Green.
Left: Eileen's 1924 Vauxhall Princeton tourer; right: her classic six-cylinder A.C. 'Ace', 1925, with George and Eva in the back

must stand as it is. It would not be fair otherwise.' Her firm but reasonable tone was rewarded, and she got the higher amount.

Excitement ran high in Harmer Green Lane at the beginning of May 1924, when a letter arrived from W. R. M. Lamb, secretary of the Royal Academy, informing the young artist that 'Her Majesty the Queen yesterday selected for purchase your dry-point "Flying Swings" (No. 1066) at the registered price of £4–14–6.' The writer asked if Eileen could send a print 'of exactly the same quality, in the same kind of frame, as it might interest the Queen to know that the work could be delivered to her without waiting for the close of the Exhibition.' A special Royal print duly went off – and to her family the artist had become a star. 'Hearty congratulations, dear girl,' wrote a cousin in May 1924. 'We indeed share the honour but are only little microbes compared to you.'

By then, at the age of nineteen, with her wide, intelligent face and waist-long cascade of shining hair, Eileen had become a strikingly attractive young woman, her looks marred only by the fact that she had inherited some of her mother's heavy bone structure about the jaw, and that her upper teeth were slightly splayed. Together, these defects gave her a faintly thuggish look. A photograph which shows her at the wheel of a fine A.C. Ace six-cylinder tourer, in 1925, says much about the structure of the family. Eileen, who had taken out a licence two years earlier, is very much in the driving seat, with Eva and her father in the back, and her mother not in evidence at all. The dog on her lap is Robin, one of several terriers owned by her father. The look on her face, if not quite challenging, at least shows determination and suggests that she would not stand much nonsense: clever, lively, competent, highly skilled with her hands, she was already an international success. (Cars played an important role in her life, and in 1936 she bought a beautiful, low-slung Riley, in which she took great delight. She loved driving, and was good at it, and chalked up mileage done on the wall of the garage. She was also a skilled mechanic, and carried out many servicing jobs herself.)

By her own account, written when she was forty, she suffered chronically from physical weakness. 'Frail health has held me back in many things,' she told a friend. 'I have never had the physique for anything vigorous. My trouble is gastric . . . we suffer from it as a family . . . I have never been one of the hale and hearty ones, and cannot work too long hours, or I crack up at once. It exasperates me when there is so much I am longing to do.'

How much of this was retrospective hypochondria? Certainly the girls took energetic exercise when they were young, playing tennis on the lower lawn and going for bicycle rides, besides walking over the fields with their father in search of subjects to sketch. Later, Eileen displayed formidable endurance watching badgers in the harshest weather, and put in long hours at her easel and her typewriter. Yet it is true that all the Sopers were natural ectomorphs, and never put on any weight, tending to become ever-thinner, the older they grew. By the end of the 1930s the family had ceased to eat meat, relying instead on fish and eggs – though whether their change of diet was dictated by nutritional or by ethical considerations, it is impossible to say. Eileen recalled that she and Eva had been forced to eat meat as children, but that she had always hated it and was better off without.

One question leaps to the mind of a biographer: why did she never marry? Among all her voluminous papers, scarcely a trace survives of any romantic interest in men. Not only did she remain a lifelong spinster: more than that, there seems to have been something in her nature that shunned every manifestation of sexuality. Once, in her forties, sending a friend a copy of Shakespeare's sonnets, she lamented the fact that the Bard should so often have descended from grace. 'I feel sure that you will like some of these as much as I do,' she wrote, 'but I am a little troubled lest any of

'Prisoners' shows early proof of Eileen's concern for wild creatures.

the, shall we say, coarse expressions in some of the others may offend you.'

In all the mass of papers she left behind, there is only one hint of romance, and this seems to refer – though the connection is by no means certain – to Eric Liddell, the Olympic sprinter, who won a gold medal in the 400 metres, and a bronze in the 200 metres, at the Games in Paris in 1924 (and the story of whose supposed rivalry with Harold Abrahams went round the world half a century later in the film *Chariots of Fire*). Certainly Liddell stayed with the Sopers as a child, for his family was connected with theirs, and he was three years Eileen's senior; later – apparently in 1925 – she painted a formal oil portrait of him, dressed in a three-piece grey suit: a rather heavy and unattractive picture. Liddell became a missionary in China, was interned by the Japanese during the second world war and died a prisoner in 1945; but for some reason Eileen left his portrait standing on the easel of her studio for several years at the end of her life – and one undated poem hints that, years ago, he had awoken some deep response in the shy young artist:

Eileen's portrait of Eric Liddell stayed permanently on the easel at Wildings to the end of her life.

To E.L.

We walked the fields of June,
When lifting skies,
Blue as the speedwell, tossed
The white clouds flying
Over the hill's rise.
There was a peewit crying.

Up, up we climbed
Till we might look
Down on the valley,
Field and brook,
Till we had gained the sunken way
By alder and by hawthorn drowned,

And in the green, leaf-chaliced gloom,
In that unwonted place we found
Solomon's seal in bloom.
I thought I saw the blossom droop
Like tears upon the spray,
But you were glad, and gay!

We walked the woods of June,
And in the tangled light
Where many names were carved
For lovers' past delight,
You wrote that Time might spell
The letters E and L,
Though loath to mar
The beauty of the tree,
Engraved them but lichen-deep
With silver key.

Progress has cleared
The sunken way.
On fallen leaves
The beech is lying.
Nothing remains of that fair day
Save a lonely peewit crying.

The older Eileen grew, the more spinsterly she became. Nobody who knew her would have dreamt of making a dirty joke in her presence, and most people who came in contact with her found themselves tailoring their conversation as to a shorn lamb. Her whole life was exceptionally sheltered – a point emphasised by consideration of things she never did: she never married, never had children, never left home, never went abroad, never swore, drank alcohol or killed any creature larger than a fly, no matter how severely it might annoy her. Only once – in the memory of anyone still living – did she express regret that her life had been so limited, and that was in 1944, when Jessie, the daughter of her former nanny, announced her engagement. 'Of course,' she said as she congratulated the bride-to-be, 'Eva and I should have left home long ago. But now it's far too late.' She was then thirty-nine, and immovably set in her routines.

Was her virginal innocence – which Eva shared – innate? Or was it compounded by the over-protective attitude of her father? In the photographs of George supervising Eileen at work in the studio, the teacher is in very close control of his pupil: his extreme proximity and intense attitude suggest that he may have been something of a martinet. Yet even if he was, Eileen never grudged it: on the contrary, she revered him.

In the summer of 1925, perhaps spurred on by him, she launched an autograph-hunt, writing to a number of well-known men and asking for their signatures. Her biggest catch came from the Reform Club in a note dated 21 July. 'Dear Madam,' it said. 'By all means! Here it is. H. Belloc.' Others who answered included the composer Roger Quilter, the poet Laurence Binyon, and 'The Man with a Million Invisible Friends!', Rex Palmer, alias Uncle Rex of the British Broadcasting Company.

Not only did Eileen draw, etch and paint: she also wrote verse. Her own love of poetry was stimulated by hearing works by John Masefield on the radio, and she read eagerly, concentrating on poets of the countryside such as John Clare and Edward Thomas. For much of her adult life, verse poured out of her, and she scribbled it down on any piece of paper that came to hand – on old envelopes, on the backs of bills, on the inside of opened-out cereal packets. Most of the poems were not very good, even though she ceaselessly

Eileen A. Soper

Opposite:
'Leapfrog' probably derives from her
visits to Camber Sands, East Sussex.

refined them, producing draft after draft: her thoughts were of birds, animals, flowers, the wind, the changing seasons, captivity and freedom, but she could rarely sustain the rhythms and lyrical expression that would have made them take wing. Only in occasional lines and phrases – 'The first sweet pain of spring' – did she strike gold.

Nevertheless, she was eager to try out her work on distinguished judges. Early in 1928 she sent a batch to W. E. Hodgson, in the hope that he would ask his brother, the poet Ralph Hodgson, to read them, and at the end of February W. E. sent back a guarded response. 'What I did glean from him,' he wrote, 'is that although you are a pretty verse writer, you are inclined to be too fluent . . . I have to stress the danger of fluency in verse-writing, and above all things, be doubly critical before you put anything out.'

Similar advice came from a still more eminent authority, the novelist John Galsworthy, then at the height of his renown, to whom Eileen had somehow obtained an introduction. 'Dear

Madam,' wrote the author of *The Forsyte Saga* from Bury House, his home near Pulborough, on 26 April 1929, 'I like the thought and feeling in the poems, but I think the expression wants more working at – it's rather ragged. You see this isn't free verse, and I think it would be better if you didn't take liberties with the length of lines and the rhythm.'

Her attitude to life was fundamentally serious, her whole existence devoted to work; although she had a good sense of humour she generally kept it well in check, especially in her writing. When she and Eva both showed themselves keen and able to join their father in his profession – when, in fact, George discovered that he had bred a whole colony of artists – he commissioned a firm of architects to design a bigger studio, which was built as an extension on the first floor of the house, at the back, directly above the original work-room. The addition gave everyone more space, and the new studio was well lit by a very large north-facing window, nine feet across and six high, with a skylight abutting the top of it, so that the area of glass continued for two feet up the slanted ceiling. Yet its design was abysmal, in that there was a gap of at least an inch

between the vertical and the sloping glass, with no means of closing it, so that in winter the room was arctically cold, and ice often formed on the inside of the panes. The original studio became a kiln-room, which housed an electrically fired kiln, a potter's wheel and an etching-press.

There, all through the 1920s and 1930s, the family worked away as a team. Eva, the least gifted of the three but clever with her hands, tried turning pottery vessels, but found the wheel too tiring and took to making figures of birds and animals, with which she had considerable success, receiving many commissions from the Royal Worcester Porcelain Company. Eileen modelled pottery children, her father horses. Account books show that Eva received modest payments from the others for making prints on their behalf – although Eileen later emphasised that, for printing his delicate wood engravings, her father never used a press, 'but undertook the tedious and highly skilled task of hand-printing each proof himself.'

Eileen herself would tour the countryside in the family car, sometimes acting as chauffeur to her father, but often searching on her own for attractive children to draw – an activity she continued even when she and Eva went off on holiday. In a joint letter sent home one August from Camber, near Rye, in Sussex, addressed to 'Dear Bloss and Dad', Eva reported that she was lying on the beach in blazing sun, and rambled on for two pages, but Eileen just added a quick note: 'I have no time to write this morning as I am prowling round for children on the sands.'

For several years her etchings continued to sell well, especially in America. She worked through the fine-art publisher and exporter H. C. Dickins, and opened an account at the Fifth Avenue Bank in New York, amassing a substantial sum of money there. Then, when the depression of the 1930s killed the demand for etchings, she followed her father's footsteps and went into book illustration.

Yet her greatest joy was to go out sketching or painting with him into the country. Surviving pictures show that they often tackled the same landscape together, sitting side by side, and later in life she wrote lyrically of their joint excursions, across fields 'covered with all kinds of meadow flowers: dog daisies, centaury, wild mint, thyme, scabious, helianthemum, many different kinds of orchids, in fact flowers innumerable.' From childhood she remembered 'many a thrilling expedition or dawn watch in the

outlying woods and fields', and sometimes the pair of artists travelled further, to sketch the different landscapes of the Sussex Downs or the East Anglian coast. Sussex captivated her above all other counties, and she never forgot a young shepherd called George Diplock, who 'could talk for hours of the downland country, its history, and such details as the making of dew-ponds, sheep-bells and shepherds' crooks'. To her the shepherd embodied 'the true essence of peace – a timeless figure whose way of life is symbolic of ease and contentment'.

For Eileen, the 1930s were and always remained a golden age, which her father's engravings and paintings caught to perfection: his prints, she felt, reflected 'the serenity that seemed then still to prevail on the land'. Mechanisation had scarcely begun to erode the age-old rituals of farming, and heavy horses were ubiquitous, pulling the plough, the harrow, the drill and the roller, hauling timber from the woods, and providing most rural power. 'Fine

39

George Soper's fine wood engravings of rural scenes were much admired by his daughter.

subjects [for her father] were on every side,' she wrote. 'A stone's throw from the garden he could usually find a ploughing team or some other field-work in progress, and farms were, in themselves, a rich source of material. Odd corners of the farmyard, buildings, particularly tithe barns ... the stacks and hay-ricks ... the woven hedges and old five-bar gates ... in harmony with nature.'

Living and working with her father in this Arcadian landscape, she became imbued with his values and ideas, and equated the integrity of the natural world with that of the artist who could represent it faithfully. Her views on the subject were traditional, forthright and absolutely rigid. 'You ask, "Do I like Modern Art?"', she once wrote to a friend. 'Most emphatically, NO! How does so much appalling rubbish get on to canvas? No – art for me must have form, good composition, and take its pattern from the beauty of nature. These men who paint a woman with a great eye in some remote section of her anatomy, five arms and ten legs, fingers like bunches of bananas, ought to be struck like it themselves. They should be put away where they can do less harm. The trouble is, they can't do a good drawing, so they try, and unfortunately succeed, in getting notoriety by doing freak work.'

Her irritation burst out in a lively take-off of Kipling's 'If' – almost the only humorous poem she ever permitted herself:

> If you can paint a tree without relation
> To foliage, form and colour Nature lent,
> If you can call the thing 'A Railway Station',
> In case they thought a tree was your intent;
>
> If you can take a lump of clay and mould it
> Into a shape no woman ever bore,
> Call in a County Council to behold it,
> And sell it for a thousand quid or more;
>
> If you can take a block of wood and scratch it
> With thin white lines that tell of nothing much,
> If you can find a publisher to match it,
> And know, my boy, you've lost the common touch;
>
> If you can paint a woman warped and twisted,
> With limbs – God help her – weighing half a ton,
> Yours is the fame, and all the praise enlisted,
> And – which is more – you'll fill the Tate, my son!

For the moment, she herself had not found a way of expressing her deep feeling for the natural world through the medium of art, and tried instead to do it through poems, with only limited success. Yet the habit of studying nature, and of depicting it, was planted deep within her.

Much practical knowledge could be gleaned from the garden, which throughout her lifetime had been gaining in interest and splendour, as the flowers, shrubs and trees which her father had planted achieved maturity, to the great advantage of the birds. To her, almost every plant had ornithological advantages or drawbacks. As a lover of nature (she wrote), her father 'often preferred the wild plant to the hybrid', and he had deliberately sited many climbing plants such as species of clematis so that they could go up trees and shrubs. She herself became a connoisseur of clematis varieties, and particularly recommended *Clematis spooneri* as a favourite nesting site for chaffinches and other birds. 'Both garden

and bird lovers will be repaid if they can glimpse a hedge-sparrow's nest and eggs among the blue clematis blossom and the pink of *Erica mediterranea*,' she wrote, and she devoted much time and effort to creating such desirable combinations. 'Most low-growing shrubs, particularly the miniature conifers, attract the hedge-sparrows, and the thick foliage gives some privacy from the cuckoo, which too often imposes on these unobtrusive little birds to rear her offspring ... The garden warbler sings incessantly in *Rosa wilmottiae*.' Loving roses, she favoured especially old-fashioned varieties, and liked to have them straggling wherever they wanted to go, not 'trimmed into the distorted horrors seen in many gardens'. A bird sanctuary, she recommended, should have plenty of berried shrubs like cotoneasters, 'for these are invaluable in attracting and feeding birds'. The big *Cotoneaster frigidus* outside her studio window brought 'a crowd of blackbirds and song- and mistle-thrushes to feed on its berries ... Lonicera berries are a favourite of the marsh tit, and you will bring joy to him and yourself if you can procure a plant of the lovely bush honeysuckle *L. pyrenaica* ... Irish yews generally give a good supply of berries, which are greatly appreciated by thrushes and fieldfares.'

Altogether, Eileen's botanical and silvicultural knowledge was impressively detailed; and the garden sanctuary became more and more important to her as the countryside round about was progressively invaded by new houses and factories. Easily the worst single innovation, from the Sopers' point of view, was the construction of an entire new town, Welwyn Garden City, which began in 1930. 'Although the building so far does not come nearer than about three miles away,' wrote Eileen to a friend, 'we fear for the future.'

The family, though not yet in thrall to animals and birds, was already much involved with them. A series of dogs began with a buff-coloured bobtail sheepdog, when the girls were small, and continued with their favourite of all, the West Highland White terrier called Robin, or Rob, who lived for ten years. Rob's successor, a Cairn terrier called Puck, really belonged to Eva, and was also greatly loved, but died at the age of only three-and-a-half, to their great distress. During his time a cock robin became so tame that he was constantly in and out of the house, and in the winter would perch on George's knee as he sat beside the fire, with Puck at his feet. So confident was this bird that he would take pine

kernels from human lips, and, as Eileen recorded, 'he used to wake me up at the crack of dawn by hopping all over the bed, and if I didn't wake up and give him a pine kernel, he would peck at my lips – which wasn't so good!'

When war came in 1939 the family stayed put, even though the house, only twenty-five miles north of London, was well within range of German bombs meant for the capital, and of the V1 flying bombs, known as Doodlebugs, whose arrival was particularly unnerving: when their noisy engines cut out they would fly silently for a few more seconds before exploding on impact. An air-raid shelter, sunk into the ground behind the house, gave the Sopers a measure of security, and during the early years of the war they spent many nights in it: they would go to bed still wearing some of their clothes, and, if the sirens sounded, leap up and rush for cover. According to Eileen, the Doodlebugs were the most alarming form of attack:

There was little time to get out to the shelter. We would hear them coming up with the most diabolical roar (the vibration of their engines shook every door and window in the house as they passed over), then sudden silence, and waiting for the *crump*, which was a most horrible wait, especially if the bomb had not already passed. They looked terrible passing at night:

Eva's irises became a feature of the garden.

the roar, the ball of flame tearing across, low to the ground. Would this one get you, or some other unfortunate soul?

Later still came the V2 rockets, but these were less frightening in that they arrived without warning. Eileen and Eva were in Hertford one morning when one exploded overhead and blew open the doors of the house outside which they were standing. But their own home and garden escaped serious damage, even though the building was often shaken, and many of its ceilings were cracked.

Yet in the middle of the war the family sustained as grievous a loss as any that the Germans could have inflicted on them. In August 1942 George Soper died of heart-failure, aged seventy. Already the house and land had been made over to his daughters; now his modest estate of £2,877 passed to Ada. No records survive to show the impact of his demise on the rest of the family, but it must surely have been devastating. He and Ada had been married for forty-five years, and throughout his daughters' lives he had lived and worked at home, teaching them, leading them, setting them an example, in intimate daily contact. Now suddenly he was gone; and with her mother already in failing health, and her sister

47

such a passive character, it was natural that Eileen, at the age of thirty-seven, should take charge of the little household. Her grief echoed poignantly in a poem which she wrote years later:

The Debt

For all the time
That is left to me,
For all my days,
Seasons shall bloom
In memory,
The birds give praise
For you who went
Your splendid way alone,
And laughed at death,
Until your laugh was thrown
On unreturning winds!

I shall not see
The morning break on English fields again,
Or hear the lark, or feel the summer rain,
Or find the spring, or any precious thing:
The early flower; the golden harvesting;
The rickyard when the colour dies away,
And one by one the stars dispel the day,
I shall not see; I shall not beauty know
Without remembering what my heart must owe,
For all my days, a debt too deep to pay:
These things I keep –
You went your splendid way!

Moments of loss and tragedy like this must have been particularly hard for Eileen, since she seems to have had practically no religious faith in which to find comfort. In all her letters, notebooks, poems and published books there is hardly an instance of the words 'God', 'Jesus', 'Christ' or 'heaven' – not even in everyday expressions like 'Thank heaven' or 'God willing'. Only once, at the start of a poem entitled 'Prayer', did she address or mention a superior power:

48

Lord, make me now
As happy as the field,
With flowers enriched . . .

Otherwise, the absence of religious thought, feeling, symbolism and language is very striking. There was, in the house, a Book of Common Prayer belonging to Ada, a Bible and a miniature edition of Hymns Ancient and Modern; but none of them showed any sign of having been used, and Eileen certainly never went to church as an adult, except for the occasional wedding of a close friend or relation. She hated Christmas, and lost no chance of decrying the festival as a waste of time and money – even though she did dutifully send out cards, usually of her own design. It is true that she never wrote an anti-religious syllable; but equally, she gave no hint that she had any private system of belief to account for the origin and purpose of life, and her own spiritual horizon seems to have been very bleak.

Four

AT THE BEGINNING of 1942 Eileen began to keep copies of her typed letters. Although she sometimes wrote by hand she generally used a portable machine, and stored carbon copies higgledy-piggledy in cardboard boxes. Her filing system – if such it can be called – was chaotic, but at least her instinct to preserve meant that she left a detailed record of her activities and gave a fascinating glimpse of her methods of work.

Even though she was primarily an artist, her urge to put words on paper was unquenchable. Poems, articles, stories and above all immensely long letters poured from her typewriter – and she seems to have realised that her verbosity was a problem, for often two copies of attempts at the same letter have survived, and always the second, the one which was sent, is shorter than the first. Her typing was accurate, and her spelling mostly good, although she clung to a few endearing eccentricities, like 'hoards of insects' and 'pouring over a newspaper'.

It seems to have been pure chance that her career as an illustrator, which had built up steadily during the 1930s, suddenly blossomed in 1941, when she began the most fruitful professional partnership of her life – with Enid Blyton. At the behest of the London publisher Macmillan she teamed up with this, the most prolific writer for children ever known, and, through her speed, accuracy, professionalism and sheer skill at matching the mood of the stories, she made herself an indispensable member of the Blyton stable for over twenty years. Sometimes in private she would confide to friends that she considered the illustration of Blyton books hack-work and a chore; sometimes also she complained that the author was a menace, in that she demanded footling alterations in drawings that were already adequate. Yet for most of the time the partnership functioned extremely well, and Miss Blyton was loud in her praise of Eileen's efficiency and draughtsmanship – as in a letter of 1948: 'Thankyou for the drawings. They are better than ever, and are quite beautiful. I really do like them enormously ... Thankyou so much for all your good work – it does make a lot of difference to an author to have her books properly illustrated.' A year later she wrote to Noel Evans, of Evans Brothers: 'I don't need to see roughs of *any* of her sketches. She and I have worked together for so long now, and I have always found her accurate and dependable – in fact excellent in every way.' Although the two women met several times, and exchanged countless letters, their relationship never became close: they remained, as they had begun, 'Dear Miss Blyton' and 'Dear Miss Soper', and they signed themselves 'Yours, Enid Blyton' and 'Sincerely Yours, Eileen A. Soper'.

Eileen's first Blytons were the first three *Readers* and *I'll Tell You a Story*, all published in 1942. In the next year she did *Merry Story Book*, *Polly Piglet* and *The Toys Come to Life*. With only seventeen books published in 1943, however, the author was barely into her stride; and when she hit better form in 1944, with twenty-two new titles, Eileen illustrated no fewer than six of them, including her first 'Fives' book, *Five Run Away Together*. Eight different

Eileen's cover design for a typical 'Famous Five' adventure

publishers handled this huge output, and Eileen seems to have worked easily with all of them. 'I am very pleased to have this opportunity of telling you how much I like your work, about which Miss Blyton and all concerned are very enthusiastic,' wrote Harry Cowdell, her main contact at Macmillan, on 1 January 1943; and her relationship with author and publishers continued on that buoyant note. Her illustrations for a series of Nature Readers, done in the summer of 1943, were judged particularly successful, and led to a commission to produce sixty wall-charts, at a fee of £8–8–0 each, to accompany the books. Her friendly relations with Cowdell led her to ask if he could find her some paint brushes better than the poor-quality ones which were all she could buy locally; and when he sent her three, which he had run to earth in Caterham, she was overjoyed. 'These are simply marvellous!' she wrote. 'They seem of pre-war quality, and I cannot imagine how you were able to get them.'

Nor was she working only for Enid Blyton. In 1943 she also illustrated Mary Moore's *Malta, a Kitten,* and then her *Moore's Rabbit Tales* (although she questioned the author's recommendation that a tame rabbit was best picked up by its ears). In all, her output of work was phenomenal, for a typical 'Fives' book needed a colour frontispiece and full-colour wrapper, two two-colour drawings for endpapers, eight full-page line drawings in two colours, and twenty-four other drawings in black only. Luckily her style, which had scarcely changed or matured since her earliest etchings, blended innocence and naïvety in exactly the right proportions to match the spirit of the Blyton stories.

Inevitably, there were occasional setbacks. 'On reading *Five Go Off to Camp,*' wrote Paul Hodder-Williams of Hodder & Stoughton, 'it seems to me that your illustration for Page 94 is not quite right. In the scene you depict, only Jock and the farmhand Peters should be in the picture. Jock had left the other children at their camp before making his way back to his home, after seeing the spook-train. As children are pretty quick on to this sort of thing, I think it would be better if you re-drew the picture ... don't you?' In similar vein Harry Cowdell pointed out: 'In *The Wonderful Conker* there should be seven blades to the horsechestnut leaves; in *The Cross Little Tadpole* would you make the tadpoles' tails more wriggly?' Later Paul Hodder-Williams suggested: 'By the way, you always write to my uncle, Percy Hodder-Williams, who retired

'Up she went like a cat'. Jo climbs the wall in Five Have a Wonderful Time *by Enid Blyton.*

about three years ago. I do not mind a bit, but you may like to alter it in your address book.'

Busy as she was with her drawing, Eileen also longed to write; and maybe it was her association with a phenomenally successful author that goaded her to finish a little illustrated book of her own for children, *Happy Rabbit*, which she submitted to Macmillan in the autumn of 1945. To her delight, they accepted it promptly – although she reacted sharply to a suggestion that they should show her typescript to Enid Blyton for an opinion. 'As we know each other so well,' she wrote on 1 November, 'I would rather this were not done, which point of view you will understand; although I would welcome any criticism or suggestions that you, or an independent reader, would care to make.' With this rebarbative idea deflected, she accepted the firm's offer of an advance of £50, and production of the book went ahead. At first Macmillan hoped to bring it out early in 1947, but shortages of paper, fuel and labour kept delaying its appearance, and it was finally published on 17 June. The story – about a rabbit building a house, getting married and having a family – was very short and simple, but the full-colour pictures had great life and jollity. 'It is an admirable looking book,' wrote Lovat Dickson of Macmillan, 'and your illustrations should win for it high praise.'

By then Eileen had completed a second children's story, initially called *The Rainbow's Secret*, later *Dormouse Awake*, the adventures of a dormouse who takes a boat down-river to the sea, presented in much the same form, with coloured illustrations. This too Macmillan accepted and published, in 1948, again with an advance of £50; and a third in similar vein, *Sail Away Shrew* – another anthropomorphic adventure story with an aquatic theme – came out in 1949. The care that the author lavished on these little books was made clear by a letter which she wrote to Harry Cowdell while the third was in production:

I enclose the corrected galleys, but I am filled with remorse. Why oh why didn't I realise that I had the nightingale singing too late in the season? The mimulus and the myosotis might, if they flowered early, manage to be out in the latter part of his singing days, but the whole story suggests summer, particularly where all those grasshoppers are sporting in the grass . . .

Eileen was thrilled to hear, in November 1949, that Queen Mary had ordered a copy of *Sail Away Shrew* – a gratifying echo of the occasion, twenty-five years earlier, when she had bought a Soper etching at the Royal Academy. But a fourth children's book, *Moles and Moonshine*, did not find favour with publishers, and, in spite of its author's energetic attempts to place it, never saw the light of day. Her persistence in trying to find publishers, for this and other stories, was extraordinary. On the backs of torn-up cereal packets she kept pencilled notes of the firms she had tried: five for *Moles and Moonshine*, two for *Castaway Squirrel*, three for *Frolic Fawn* and no fewer than sixteen for a story about a pig called *Minikin's Mischief*.

She would have saved much time and effort if she had employed a literary agent, but although several people suggested that she should engage one, she always fought against the idea. One reason was that, being careful about money, she grudged the ten per cent of her earnings that an agent would take; but, apart from that, she was inhibited by some bad experience she had had with an American agent before the war. A third reason was that she hoped she might herself be able to exploit her own early success in the United States. Not only had her etchings made a hit there in the 1920s: during the war, the *Christian Science Monitor* had published several poems and articles in which she extolled America's contribution to the struggle against Hitler, and praised the admirable qualities of the US servicemen whom she had met in England.

Thus when she came to sign the contract for *Happy Rabbit*, she made a special arrangement whereby she retained the American rights. 'Since I have a market of long standing in the States,' she wrote, 'I would prefer to be free to handle the American rights myself.' Later, when Macmillan in New York declined to publish the book, and the London firm suggested that she should use the agents Curtis Brown, she again side-stepped their recommendation, on the same grounds. This mistrust of agents never left her, and she rejected several overtures from the New York firm Arthur North – almost certainly to her own detriment, for she over-estimated the power of her name in America, where her reputation was that of an artist, rather than a writer.

Eileen A. Soper

Geranium subcaulescens.

The urge to write poems burned with equal strength, and by November 1945 she had amassed enough to offer Macmillan a collected volume, entitled *The Fledgling and Other Poems*. But the firm rejected it, with the observation that although the book contained 'some pleasing nature lyrics', the majority were 'rather slight'. Undaunted, she began offering poems to the magazine *Country Life* – the first salvo of an irregular bombardment that she kept up intermittently for several years, occasionally scoring a hit and breaking into print, but having most of her shots gently deflected. The splendidly named Literary Editor, Brenda Spender, soon had her measure, and showed herself to be a mistress of emollient evasion. 'I like these, but have so much spring poetry in type that I have had to decide to take no more this year ... This is a nice piece of work, but a little difficult, I feel. You know that I always love reading your work and should probably take this, but have too much in type ... Thankyou very much for letting me see these poems, both very attractive, but not quite my choice ... They are very delightful, but just don't force me to take them at a time when I have too much.'

Chiff-chaffs and (opposite) long-tailed tits

From time to time Eileen also submitted articles to *Country Life*, and had one on dormice accepted; but when she tried the magazine with a piece on hornets she met with a nasty rebuff. 'It is written too much from the amateur point of view, and asks questions which I would normally expect the contributor to *Country Life* to answer,' thundered Frank Whitaker, the Editor, who was building the magazine up from its low war-time level. 'I am naturally in constant touch with several leading entomologists, and there is really no reason why I should publish a speculative article on the insects when I could very easily get an authoritative article from them.'

It would have been only natural if Eileen had countered this rebuke with a waspish answer; in fact she replied mildly, remarking on how difficult it was to find good information about hornets – whereupon Whitaker sought to defend his ground with the unanswerable observation: 'I have looked farther into the articles we have published about hornets, and I find that there were two in 1944, both by Colonel Buzzard.'

Eileen had better luck with *Songs on the Wind*, a volume of children's verse, together with illustrations, which she offered to the publisher Robert Hale at the end of 1945, emphasising in her covering letter that good reproduction of the drawings 'would, of course, be essential'. Hale, though professing to like the book 'very much indeed', said that his mass of prior commitments meant that he would not be able to publish it for two years at least, and he passed it on to his associated company, Museum Press, who specialised in children's works, and who accepted it with enthusiasm.

Little did they realise what a demanding author they had taken on. They must have sensed, from the extreme length of her letters, that she might cause problems, but they can hardly have foreseen how exacting she would prove. At first everything went well; then Eileen made it clear that she meant to have a hand in the production of the book. 'It is not what I would have liked,' she wrote, when the publishers sent her a sample of blue binding cloth in April 1946, 'but it seems we shall have to have this as there is no other available.' In July, encouraged by the fact that they had accepted *Songs on the Wind* so promptly, she tried them with her rejected volume of adult verse, now called *Hedgerows' Harvest*; but this they rejected, on the grounds that their sales department could not foresee a large enough market to make publication worthwhile.

Production of the children's book went slowly ahead. In September Eileen returned the paste-up with a 700-word letter that began, 'You will see that I have made some small adjustments', and in November did much the same with the proofs. Yet it was in January 1947, when she saw a proof of the jacket, that trouble really set in. 'I am sorry,' she wrote to Arthur Morris, one of the firm's directors, 'but I am most distressed by it. I had no idea there was any question of having to use one of the blues from the illustration. All the value of the colour scheme in the picture is lost, and the result is unendurable to my artistic sense ... I can't tell you how disappointed I am.'

She was not just being difficult: it was the artist in her speaking. 'I have put all I know into this book,' she added, 'and I do feel so strongly on this point.' A dispute broke out about who should pay the extra costs incurred by the changes she was demanding. She invoked a 'printer friend' to side with her, and slow aesthetic arguments rumbled on for months. 'I have discussed the progressive proofs for the jacket with my printer friend,' she wrote in April, 'and he suggests the only thing that can be done is to cut the blue block in order to separate the background from the pictures, and print it in a fifth colour ... It is regrettable that

57

apparently no attempt was made by the blockmaker to attain the correct blue in the first place ... As you do not feel you can go to the cost of the extra printing, I have no alternative but to do so myself, as to print the jacket in its present state would be detrimental to my reputation.'

After a lull, the dispute flared up again in January 1948, with volleys of letters in both directions. 'I am sorry, but I could never agree to the publication of the jacket in a form so alien to my own conception of colour,' wrote Eileen on the 28th, when she had seen the latest version; and even when she got a finished copy of it, in March, she reacted querulously: 'I cannot understand your saying the colour "exactly matched" my specimen. I thought directly I saw it that it was not right ... it would be a disaster were they to print all the jackets like this.'

When at last she saw a finished copy of the book, in April 1948, she was to some extent mollified. She agreed that the binding cloth was 'very nice indeed', in both colour and texture, and that the endpapers were well produced; but still she found fault with the reproduction of the black-and-white drawings and suggested that, if there were to be a reprint, she might go and talk to the printers first.

Songs on the Wind eventually came out in September 1948, priced 7s 6d (37½p). The book born after such labour was – it must be said – a very modest production, barely fifty pages long. The curly-haired children that featured in its drawings were babyish and saccharine-sweet, and its poems – mainly on rural subjects – were workmanlike rather than memorable, tending to be blighted by the lack of spontaneity evident in the verse that dedicated the book to the author's father:

> One dew-wet morning filled with song
> He led my early steps along,
> Among the meadow flowers to stand,
> A pencil in my eager hand.

At the end of November Museum Press reported that they had sold about 1000 copies, but that demand was 'not as brisk' as they could wish, and they were very glad when, in January 1949, the Macmillan company of New York agreed to buy 500 bound copies. Yet the muted reception that the book received did nothing to dampen Eileen's enthusiasm for writing.

Five

Dɴ the final months of the war Eileen had opened up two important new friendships, both postal, both transatlantic. The first was with Elizabeth O'Connor Ledbetter, an American poet who lived in Jacksonville, Florida, and the second was with Henry Greene, a naturalist, gardener and bird enthusiast who wrote from his home at Petersham, Massachusetts. Both correspondents had been attracted by her work: Elizabeth had seen an illustrated article entitled 'Thankyou, America', which appeared in the *Christian Science Monitor* magazine in April 1943, and Henry had bought several of Eileen's etchings during a trip to England during the 1920s. After a cautious start her feelings towards this diverse and far-flung pair warmed rapidly. 'Dear Mr Greene' soon became 'My Dear Henry', and within a few weeks Eileen was signing off not with 'Yours sincerely' but with 'Our love to everyone. As always, Yours.' Towards Elizabeth she became still more affectionate. Formal opening exchanges gave way to 'My Dearest Elizabeth', and closing salutations advanced rapidly until Eileen was writing, 'Our fondest love and kindest thoughts for you all, As always in friendship, yours lovingly.'

A cynic might say that it was the food parcels sent by both parties which elicited such heartfelt replies; and certainly, generous packages of goods no longer available in England – fruit juice, tinned peaches, cream, flour, biscuits, raisins, tuna fish, jam, chocolate, maple syrup, dried apricots – poured into Harmer Green from both the Greene and the Ledbetter households. When Elizabeth sent a new raincoat, and Henry stockings, Eileen wallowed in superlatives as she struggled to express her overwhelming gratitude. Yet her response was provoked by far more than mere thankfulness. Somehow the interest in her life and work shown by two friendly but distant strangers encouraged her to open up and talk

Missel thrush

to them on paper with a freedom that she found impossible when face to face with people.

Her closest relationship was with Elizabeth, for whom, in due course, she illustrated a book of verse. A shared interest in poetry, and mutual admiration of each other's work, led to the exchange of many confidences. 'I feel I know you so much better,' she wrote in February 1946, after the American had sent a photograph of herself. 'I can see a very kind and sympathetic nature in your expression, which is beautiful. What nice curly hair you have: it is so becoming, and I wish I had it.' She herself sent snaps in return, and when Elizabeth wrote 'I love the way you look: a face that is strong, highly intelligent, understanding and sensitive too,' she answered deprecatingly, 'Thankyou for the compliment you pay me. But I'm afraid the snaps must be deceptive, as I am just a Plain Jane.' In April she wrote, 'I should indeed love to meet you, and I know I should like you, for you have so much sympathy and understanding – qualities all too rare now. And we have so much in common. My fear would be that you would be disappointed in me!' To this Elizabeth replied, 'Oh, my dear, never would I be disappointed in you. That I know full well. I have seen your real self, your soul, in your work. You are beautiful to me.'

Galvanised by such heady thoughts, in June Eileen urged: 'If you do have any [more photographs] taken, do let me see one, for I cannot see very much of you in the snaps. I do wish so many miles did not divide us. We could have such lovely times together.' Later in the month she exclaimed: 'What a kind friend you are! I would say you are one in a million.' Then in July: 'Yes, ours is a happy friendship, for ... I love so much that you love. In fact we have the same or similar loves.' In October, after Elizabeth had again praised her, she made a deprecating response: 'You pay me far too high a compliment, and I am afraid I fall very much below your beautiful conception of me.'

What made Eileen, at the age of forty, open up so candidly to a woman whom she had never met? Clearly she was moved by intense feeling. Yet the most remarkable feature of her correspondence was its size. From the second half of 1945, all through 1946 and most of 1947 her output of letters was immense. Always typing, always keeping a carbon copy, she often wrote to Elizabeth twice in a week, and to Henry the same: four letters, single-spaced, of at least two pages each, often of three or four pages – and this on top of the mountain of other work that she had in hand. Since one of her constant refrains was that she was frantically busy, and could never find time to do half the things she wanted, this huge extra output of up to 8000 words a week can only have been a form of self-indulgence and therapy, an emotional release, an outpouring of remarks and ideas that she was unwilling or unable to try on anyone close at hand.

Much of it, as she herself acknowledged, was simply chatter – and indeed she referred to her own epistles as 'chats'. She wrote one sitting in the back seat of her Riley as she waited for the car to be serviced, with the typewriter on her knees, and between remarks about the black-market in new and second-hand vehicles gave reports on mechanical progress: 'The garage son has now decided the oil needs changing, so I shall have to wait for that.' Often such news as she had became interspersed by asides about her immediate surroundings: 'A halt there to feed a cock chaffinch, who came and perched on my hand. They do not mind the clatter of the typewriter, and come on the table beside it.'

From the letters there emerge many illuminating details of life in the Soper household at the end of the war. In general, the family saw themselves as upper or upper-middle class, a cut above ordinary Hertfordshire villagers. In conversation they referred to their part-time gardener as 'Bland' rather than as 'Harold', and before the war little Jessie Bland – Harold's niece, and the daughter of their nanny/housekeeper Annie – had never been allowed to play

in their garden except when the family was on holiday. One day, after being shown round the grounds of Knebworth House by its owner, Lord Lytton, Eileen remarked to Elizabeth:

Perhaps what would have struck you as strange was to walk round with a man to whom it was natural to be greeted by the dairy maid with 'Good evening, My Lord' ... To me there is something pleasant in this form of address, since it retains something of the old dignity that has always been the backbone of England.

Natural Conservatives, the Sopers were profoundly shaken by the Labour victory and the overthrow of Winston Churchill in the General Election of July 1945. Eileen hated the Socialists: she lost no opportunity to pour scorn on their incompetence and bigotry, and soon was writing:

I begin to wish we could leave here and live in the States – a thing I had never thought to wish for, as I love Britain so dearly. But this Government is going to make our lives wretched if it remains in power. We are to be forced to do just as they wish, in every way. Our freedom will be entirely lost ... We have a few raspberries in the garden, but they will not let us purchase a length of wire-netting to keep them from the birds. Yet they keep crying 'Grow more food!' I suppose they think you are a Capitalist if you own a few raspberry canes.

For one so deeply buried in the country, Eileen had a surprisingly strong interest in politics, and several times wrote to Harold Macmillan (who, besides being a Member of Parliament, and later Prime Minister, was Chairman of the publishing house). Once she even offered to design a poster for a Conservative election campaign.

By 1945 Ada, or Blossom, was already a background figure, described by Eileen as 'very frail', and much given to knitting, but otherwise contributing little to the household economy: in fact she was becoming rather eccentric, and tended to pull up flowers under the impression that they were weeds. Her two daughters shared a bedroom, as they always had, and were 'such close companions'

that Eileen could not imagine them living apart. Eva did all the cooking, and, hampered though she was by rationing and the lack of basic foodstuffs, she always made the bread. Outside, she supervised the vegetable garden, growing tomatoes in a small greenhouse, and in the autumn she put much effort into bottling a supply of them for the winter. Her horticultural speciality was the hybridisation of irises, at which she excelled, producing a strain with unusual blue beards. Sometimes in Eileen's letters she sounds almost a slave, toiling away in the kitchen while her sister writes to her American friends: 'I must go now, as Eva has supper nearly ready.'

If Eva was the family's breadmaker, Eileen was its breadwinner, earning a good income by illustrating books and articles, and, more and more, by writing books of her own. Sometimes in fine weather she took her typewriter out into the garden, but otherwise she worked in the studio. She also drove the car, did the shopping, led occasional expeditions to London and generally conducted affairs.

To help them in the house the sisters still had Annie, now married to Bertie Bland, who worked on a nearby farm, but she came in for only two days a week, and the Sopers found it a struggle to keep the house in order. Already the studio was in chaos. 'Oh the hunts I have sometimes when a letter or some other wanted thing gets snowed under in the studio!' Eileen wrote in October 1945. 'I've such a crowd of stuff in here, and it's like looking for a needle in a haystack.'

In summer the house was comfortable enough, but in winter it was wretchedly cold and awkward, especially when fuel rationing added to their privations. There was no central heating, and at least three fires had to be lit every morning – in the studio, the living-room and the hot-water boiler, which could not be stoked up overnight because coal was in such short supply. In the studio, before the fire took effect, the room was often so cold that ice formed inside both the north window and the skylight, and Eileen had to work muffled in coats and sheepskin boots. She repeatedly described the room as an 'ice well'.

Outside, things were better. Even after neglect during the war, the garden gave immense pleasure, and Eileen eagerly exchanged botanical information with Henry, himself a keen grower of flowers and vegetables, who sent over seeds of squash, giant tomatoes, morning glory and other plants. 'Did I tell you I had bought a

little plant of *Houstonia goerlules*?' asked Eileen in May 1946. 'One of your natives, isn't it? It is blooming well and looking so lovely. I meant to ask you whether you could find me a pinch of seed from your wild violet *Viola bicolor*. It is such a beauty, and we used to grow it here ...' When he sent over some seeds of white violet, she wrote back:

> This white one you enclose is very lovely. It is similar to the one that grows here in the garden, although ours has more mauve veining on it. I believe it is *V. striata* ... We have all sorts of violet species in the garden, among them some·very bright yellow ones. In the early spring the wild white *Viola odorata* is lovely. It seeds itself in the wild banks of the garden and has a wonderful perfume. Then we have great drifts of mauve violets, not so perfumed, sheets of them ...

Flowers were extremely important to Eileen: loving their colour, shape, texture and scent, she was infinitely curious about varieties new to her, and immensely loyal to those that her father had cultivated. She painted many careful studies of individual blooms, and in the depths of winter gathered sprays of *Chimonanthus fragrans,* the 'Winter Sweet', a Chinese shrub with a scent so powerful that a few twigs were enough to perfume the house.

With her mind focused so firmly on the natural world, she responded strongly to changes of season. 'There is always a great uplift in the spring,' she told Elizabeth, 'and for me a depression in the autumn. All the beauty of its gold cannot repay for the loss of the happier time of year.' Again and again in her poems she returned to spring, with its unfathomable mixture of happiness and pain:

> There was a morning
> Springs gone by
> When first I heard
> The cuckoo cry
> In sunshine after rain,
> And all my spirit rose to meet,
> Over the rain-soaked grass to greet,
> The ever-new surprise.
>
> I wait now half in joy,
> Half dread,
> To hear his voice again,
> Knowing its beauty hard to bear,
> And pray they will not come again
> Together, bird and rain.

When Elizabeth praised her enthusiasm, she replied, 'I used to be a very enthusiastic person, but as one goes on, one meets so many disappointments and frustrations in life' – and often her letters, though cheerful enough, have as their counterpoint a sense of strain, brought on by the fact that there was always far too much to do.

Her attitude to gardening was ambivalent. On the one hand, she wanted to maintain some sort of order, so that flowers could flourish and not be over-run by weeds. On the other, she craved wildness, and did not want the place so manicured that it would not support insects, birds and animals. One day, as she chatted to Henry on her typewriter out of doors, Harold the part-time gardener was cutting the grass with a motor-mower. 'I suppose it looks all the better for a cut,' she wrote, 'although I always hate to see the daisies mown off. Part of our lawn was a mass of blue and white, with the daisies and a little Veronica named *filiformis* (a lovely

blue), which is a perfect plague. It spreads everywhere, and is impossible to eradicate. It smothers everything.'

That summed up her dilemma exactly – and the gardener was often exasperated by contradictory instructions. 'A patch of teasels must be left to go to seed for the goldfinches,' she once wrote. 'Grass must remain uncut for the benefit of ground-nesting birds; stinging nettles left standing as cover for the blackcaps, which nest in the bramble and wild-rose thickets beyond.' Eileen was always convinced that, if her back was turned for an instant, Harold would create havoc. 'How he hates leaving those wild patches for the birds!' she wrote one May.

He likes to go round with his scythe and 'baggin 'ook' and make a clean sweep of everything, and we are terrified lest he should sweep down some of the birds' nests. The warblers build such frail little cradles, either under the grass tussocks or in the light herbage and nettles. We will not have them disturbed, and every spring and early summer we have the tussle of keeping the gardener in hand!

Life at Harmer Green – work and play alike – was severely impeded by the owners' enslavement to living creatures. 'What a nuisance a soft heart can be!' lamented Eileen. 'Particularly when it prevents one from setting the very necessary mousetraps.' A mouse, she explained, had chewed a hole through the wainscoting in the studio, and because she feared it might eat its way into some valuable book or print she had blocked the hole with cement, 'fervently hoping that the visitor was away at the time'. When she was a child, the family had kept chickens, but now, even though they depended heavily on eggs, and found it hard to get any in the lean days after the war, they could never bring themselves to have hens, because, as Eileen explained, they would be too soft-hearted to kill off old birds which could no longer lay.

Struggling to rip out the ground-ivy that threatened to stifle all other plants, Eva and the gardener were constantly held up by the discovery of toads. 'Eva is so afraid of hurting one in raking it up,' Eileen reported. 'Each one has to be carefully covered up, and his whereabouts are usually marked with a stick, lest he is disturbed again.' The one species against which Eileen was prepared to take violent action was cats. As a girl, she had loved cats; but now that

they threatened her beloved birds, she would hustle them out of the garden as fast as she could make them go – and indeed once injured her arm and shoulder quite severely in the effort of hurling a stick at some feline intruder.

Birds grew to know the sisters so well that they became importunate in their demands for food, battering on the windows in winter, and sometimes taking liberties few other admirers would have allowed:

Eva and I were taking it easy on sun loungers in the garden [Eileen reported one Easter], when a great tit flew down and tried to peck out some of Eva's hair, to line her nest. Getting shooed away, she came over to me, hopped along the rest at the back of my head, and pecked and pulled and pulled some more at my hair. I stayed still just to see what she would do. Having gathered a beakful, away she went to line her nest!

'You should have been here yesterday,' she told a friend on another occasion. 'I walked out into the garden with milled cheese on top of my head! Several long-tailed tits perched there feeding, also blue tits and robins.'

One autumn the sisters found themselves threatened with invasion. 'What amounts to a crisis has arisen in regard to the birds,' Eileen told Henry:

We are now having to keep all our windows shut, as they have taken to coming in and attacking our books, furniture, in fact any and everything they can make a hole in with their beaks! Nothing is safe any longer. I never knew birds do this. They stand on the end of my bed at the crack of dawn and hammer, hammer with their sharp little beaks till they make holes in the wood. If we leave our bedroom window open, we find book covers pecked right through the binding, cardboard boxes drilled into, paper packages torn and ripped open . . . Of course they are delightfully tame, and it is a joy having them so, but one has to draw the line at that sort of thing. We got a bit desperate this week, so bought some net curtain and fixed it up over the open window, as we do not like sleeping with our windows shut. No use! They found a little space between the net and the window-frame, and in they squeezed. About half

a dozen birds flying round your room and hopping all over you at that hour isn't very restful!

In the garden, crops were ravaged by marauders of every kind. Voles and mice ate the peas, birds the raspberries and cherries, and squirrels the walnuts, leaving the humans 'a few crumbs from the squirrels' table'. Yet Eileen would not think of having a cat, which would have had many a field-day among the trusting birds, for she could not harm any of the creatures tormenting her. Even insects escaped retribution. 'I wonder if you have slugs four or five inches long,' she asked Elizabeth. 'Hoards [*sic*] of them come out here in the evenings.' To Henry she confided:

The other evening Eva complained that her *Iris tectorum* were being devoured, so we went out with a torch and found about two dozen of these enormous snails and slugs. We gathered them all up in a flower-pot and deposited them on a piece of waste-ground in a nearby field. They will probably come back! We can't bring ourselves to tread on those great monsters, so they have to be banished to the field or thrown over the hedge to our neighbour's. We toss them lightly over the hedge, and always hope the neighbour will not get one down her neck!'

In general, the Sopers found life a struggle, and their efforts to survive were symbolised by the saga of the cherry tree that grew outside the studio window. In the old days their father had made delicious jam from its fruit – cherry jam was his speciality – and now, unable to buy fruit elsewhere, the sisters were keen to make some for themselves. The tree was too big to net, but when birds began to eat the cherries Eileen managed to pull down two small branches and cover them with muslin – only to see the airborne invaders peck holes in the muslin and devour everything inside, aided and abetted by a grey squirrel, which also penetrated the defences. So the salvage operation failed and yet another crop was lost – a minor disaster that typified the sisters' unending tussle with their environment. Lacking the vision, the resolve and the resources to do things properly – for instance, to install central heating, to reglaze the studio window or take on a full-time gardener – they lurched from one crisis to the next, tackling each new problem in the same low-geared and ineffective manner.

A woman so dedicated to preserving life naturally had strong views on shooting and hunting. Both appalled Eileen. 'I don't know what I should do if I had to bar those awful people shooting the deer,' she wrote to Henry in January 1946:

I should put up notices, MAN TRAPS, BOOBY TRAPS, YOU TRESPASS HERE AT YOUR OWN RISK – *and* I would lay the traps, too. I loathe hunting. Here, where they hunt the poor wretched foxes . . . they hunt with a pack of dogs and themselves on horseback. They are horrible people who think the country belongs to them, and they can go where they please. They had better not try coming across our garden, or they will find themselves faced by women with pitchforks. It is a cruel and vile pastime for which there is no defence.

Six

ONE CREATURE EXERCISED a greater tyranny over the household than any other: the cairn terrier Tigger. Evidently Eileen felt slight guilt about the way in which he had joined the family, for several times over, and at length, she explained to her American contacts what had happened.

The dog was born next door, but the Sopers' neighbour, a woman of uncertain temperament, neglected him as a puppy, sometimes petting him, sometimes not allowing him near her. The result was that he constantly came through the fence between the properties and cast himself at Eileen's feet: as she put it, 'he spent all his days here, and had to be returned to his owner every night'. Shuttled from one house to the other, he received no training when young, and 'of course got terribly out of hand'. His nervous temperament was exacerbated by his owner's noisy son, who 'came home for school holidays to excite and irritate him'. By the time the woman at last agreed to sell him he was 'a nervous wreck, hysterical and quite uncontrollable', with 'a crazy desire to bite all wheels, from bicycle to railway engine'. But of course the Sopers 'hadn't the heart to refuse, for we had grown to love him so much'. In fact, wrote Eileen, he was like a child to them.

So wild was the dog that they had to wire in their entire garden to keep him at home, and even though Eileen did her best to train him she never dared let him off the lead when she took him for walks, for fear that he would make a mad rush for the railway line. Even inside the garden he was frequently a menace – not least when squirrels came raiding the walnut tree. 'They nearly drive Tigger crazy,' Eileen told Henry, 'as he cannot get at them – and incidentally, his shrieks of fury nearly drive *us* mad':

There is a willow tree, a large limb of which has partially fallen,

Tigger

Eileen A. Soper

and which leans out at a precarious angle. Up this Tigger
rushes after the squirrels till he can climb no further; turns
round and rushes down again, does two or three circuits round
the tree, and back up the branch again. I think we shall have
to wire the branch to stop him doing this, or he might fall and
injure himself.

This beloved, infuriating animal – who used also to go berserk
at the sight of water flowing from a hose – had Eileen absolutely
in thrall. He might lie on her feet while she worked, but at least
once a day he had to be taken for a walk, and loud were her
complaints about how he dragged her headlong across country. 'If
for any reason I cannot take him, he creeps into a corner with his
tail down and shivers all over,' she told Elizabeth. 'He looks a most

pitiful object, and it is quite heartbreaking to leave him behind . . . So I have to be pulled all the way out for a walk, then, as he doesn't want to come back, I have to do the pulling home.'

Learning that Henry had a dog called Jigger, Tigger began to send 'wet licks', 'tail-wags' and other embarrassing messages across the Atlantic. So neurotic was he, and such did his hold over his mistress become, that he had the effect of pinning the whole family down. Plans to take a holiday were frequently scrapped because the dog could not be left behind, and even day-excursions were deemed impossible for the same reason. Once when they did take him to the sea, at Frinton on the Essex coast, there was such a fracas that they vowed never to do it again. As they sat eating their picnic lunch on the beach, 'all of a sudden there was a great WUFF from the other side of the breakwater', and three huge dogs came galloping by:

What a shemozzle! Tigger shrieked and yapped and fought to get away after them, so that they came racing up to see what it was all about, and Eva had to shoo them off as best she could, while I hung on to Tigger – which feat I began to feel was beyond me, for he is so strong when he is after another dog. He just shrieked and shrieked with frustration. Poor little thing – it seemed such a shame not to be able to let him off the lead . . . but we dare not let him run off on a strange beach. I am sure he would just run on and on in his excitement, and we should never find him again.

Next time they made an expedition to the coast they left the dog in the charge of Harold, and needless to say he was perfectly happy. These excursions to the sea were Eileen's greatest delight. The sight of the ocean awoke immortal longings in her, she told Elizabeth ecstatically.

How I love water! I can't tell you what a thrill I had out of it. The incredible beauty of the colour and the translucent movement of it all fascinate me beyond words. Oh, the scent of it all, too! How we enjoyed ourselves. We took our lunch and tea along, and were on the beach for six precious hours. Then home we turned. It is a 72-mile journey, but it was worth it. I was like a child, for I paddled in and out of the sea, sitting

Above:
Leveret

Opposite:
Running hares　　73

between whiles in the sun. Eva paddled too ... We went out like lilies and came back like petunias! My legs and feet were absolutely fried! I was able to do some sketching, for it is a fine place for children. They looked so lovely, particularly the little curly-haired babes which sat among the tiny wavelets with their little pink selves reflected underneath.

At home, apart from working on her books and illustrations, Eileen was also painting portraits, and among her sitters in the early 1950s was seven-year-old Alison Earle, whose grandmother lived at the top of Harmer Green Lane. Alison felt a special affinity with Eileen, because both of them were red-haired, and she remembered the artist as the kindest and gentlest person she had ever met, with a particular knack of accepting children and talking directly to them, but at the same time rather distant and aloof. As she worked, the windows of the studio stood open all the time, and birds flew in and out to help themselves from a pile of nuts on a work-surface. Afterwards Eileen inscribed copies of her children's books with fulsome messages: 'With special love for Alison, my little artist friend who sat so splendidly.'

That Eileen's letters carried undertones of stress is hardly surprising, for she worked extremely hard. Her mother, who had a little capital of her own, besides what George had left her, must have had a small income from investments, but Eva's earnings were modest, and it was principally on Eileen's pencil, brushes and pen that they all depended. Luckily, she did very well; even if her writing brought in little, her illustrations made a considerable amount. Her earned income fluctuated widely, but for 1950 it amounted to £2,150; and against it, to reduce income-tax liabilities, she always offset her working expenses, most of which derived from travelling in her car. She also developed a shrewd interest in investments, keeping a close eye on the stock market, and moving money around with energy and resource. 'I like the idea of making a quick profit: it would be very useful,' she once wrote to her stockbrokers, T. T. Curwen, in London, and she often asked whether a particular share would be a good buy. Sometimes she was disappointed – as when she wrote: 'The drop in En Tout Cas is a great blow to me, as I particularly wanted to sell, and the hoped-for profit was much needed'; but generally she did well, and the value of her portfolio increased steadily. The elaborately produced annual reports of the companies in which she held shares came in handy as files and scrapbooks: in the spaces left blank by avant-garde typographers she would scribble notes and outlines of ideas, sometimes continuing her scrawls on top of the type of the text itself. She was also an early investor in Premium Savings bonds, of which she bought £100-worth in 1957, and another £200-worth three years later.

To anyone who corresponded with her she seemed perfectly normal. Her letters were unfailingly logical, and, even if she was annoyed, polite. Moreover, she almost always dealt with incoming post immediately, and if even a few days elapsed before she got round to replying, she would begin, 'I am shocked to find that your letter has lain so long unanswered . . .' The few outsiders who visited her at home were enchanted by the garden, and by the sisters' extraordinary rapport with birds: Harry Cowdell, whom they entertained to lunch in the summer of 1947, went away delighted with the home-grown tomatoes they had pressed on him, and wrote warmly to say how much he had enjoyed his visit.

Yet to one or two people who saw them more often it was clear that Eileen had become the prisoner of some very odd ideas, and that Eva, following her lead, entertained similar delusions. The strangest was their phobia about cancer, which had grown from the childhood fear of germs instilled by their father until, by the end of the 1940s, it had become an obsession. So terrified were they of cancer that they could not bring themselves to name it, but referred to it in hushed voices as 'the Dread Disease', and their fear of it was such as to impose severe restrictions on their lives. Believing – in spite of frequent assurance to the contrary – that cancer was spread by airborne germs, and could be caught as easily as a common cold, they became extremely reluctant to use public transport, to frequent any public place, to enter other people's houses, or even to let any stranger enter theirs. This meant they stayed at home more and more, discouraging callers as much as

75

possible, and that any expeditions they did undertake had to be made in Eileen's car. 'Of course, we'll have to drive,' they would say when planning a trip, 'because there's always the possibility of encountering the Dread Disease.'

Occasionally in her letters to America Eileen hinted that she had become more retiring, but always she camouflaged the reclusive nature of her habits by ascribing them to some mundane cause. Thus, when telling Elizabeth how much she depended on her car, she wrote, 'I am not able to get about very well on buses and trains – my inside is not built for it!' Again, reporting that she had ceased to go to the hairdressers, she said it was because 'I just can't stand waiting . . . it takes some time to get there, and always seems such a slow business.'

Elizabeth could not know what lay behind these bland evasions; but nobody felt the force of the sisters' obsession more powerfully than Marguerite Roe, a social welfare-worker and visitor and teacher of the blind, who, through a friend, met the Sopers in 1948, and over the next few years came to know them well. From the first she was fascinated by them, and counted it a rare privilege to be taken into the secret garden, where birds would alight on her shoulders and feed from her hand, stranger though she was. Not many visitors, she knew, were so lucky, for the sisters were painfully shy, and allowed as few people as possible into the garden, so as not to disturb its occupants.

In spite of her soft red hair, blue eyes and fresh complexion, Eileen, in her mid-forties, struck Marguerite as 'not in the least pretty – in fact rather plain'. Eva, she thought, was the more attractive, and very gentle, but also 'terrified of life'. In due course Marguerite found herself invited to supper, and after a while the invitations became regular. She would go every Saturday night; the meal, cooked by Eva, was always exactly the same: very good scrambled eggs, and hot tomatoes, tinned or perhaps bottled. On summer evenings, when the windows were open, birds would fly in to join them at the table; and once as Marguerite arrived in the winter Eileen invited her to come and see 'something exciting' in the spare bedroom. Peeling back the quilt, she revealed a little pool of dormice, lying deep asleep.

These regular visits went on for a year or so; but then one evening Eva suddenly said, 'I'm sorry, but I must ask you not to come to supper any more.' Her excuse was that she was becoming arthritic, and found the extra work of entertaining a guest too arduous; but Marguerite soon discovered from her friend that this was only a cover. The real reason was more sinister. The Sopers, realising that her work sometimes put her in contact with people who were ill, had convinced themselves that she must be, or might be, contaminated by cancer germs, and so was a potential threat to them. Thereafter they never invited her to a meal again; but, so illogical was their phobia, they still welcomed her to the house now and then – particularly when they were in trouble.

One morning a letter fell through their letterbox on to the doormat. Both of them were immediately terrified, for they could see by the writing that it came from their cousin Muriel, who had the Dread Disease. Unable to touch the envelope, they picked it up with the coal tongs and laid it on the stone hearth. Then, having burnt the doormat, they telephoned Marguerite for help. 'Open it,' they said in shaking voices when she arrived; and they watched in horror as she slit the envelope. The letter turned out to be a courageous account of how the patient was faring, and Marguerite said to the sisters, 'Don't you feel privileged to have a relative who can write so bravely in these circumstances?' But Eileen and Eva simply exclaimed, 'Oh – we can't bear to think about it. Don't say another word.' So Marguerite took the letter and burnt it in the boiler; and afterwards she realised that the Sopers had used her as cannon-fodder, supposing her to be already doomed by her inevitable contacts with cancer elsewhere.

To friends such as Marguerite it seemed a terrible irony that Tigger, the beloved child-substitute, should himself fall victim to the Dread Disease. Late in 1952 he developed a limp, which at first the vet diagnosed as rheumatism; but then a lump came up on his right flank, at the back of his ribs, and the growth increased inexorably in size until, in Marguerite's vivid phrase, the dog seemed to be on the outside of it, rather than vice-versa. Faced with the inescapable fact that Tigger had cancer, the sisters reacted in the only way their phobia would allow – by rejecting him. For Marguerite it was intensely poignant and upsetting to see the poor creature, who had been petted and pampered all his life, suddenly bewildered by being pushed away with agitated cries of 'NO!' When she herself helped him on to her lap – to which he could no longer climb – Eileen was appalled.

Eileen with Tigger

For once she expressed real emotion on paper; normally her writing was controlled to the point of being wooden, but now she opened her heart to Henry Greene and his wife Bertha:

> It is unthinkable, and our world is shattered. He means so much to us. He is like a child to Eva and me. Forgive me, I can't write any more ... Our love to you both. As ever, affectionately, Eileen.

Eventually, in July 1953 – much too late – she succumbed to the inevitable and had Tigger put down. Telling Elizabeth that she would never have another dog, 'or a pet of any kind again', she wrote: 'We loved him very dearly, and it was and still is a dreadful heartbreak.' Luckily for her she was by then deeply involved in a project that had given her life a new sense of purpose, and this went some way towards taking her mind off the tragedy.

Seven

EILEEN NEVER FORGOT the thrill of seeing her first badger. It was in April 1951, and she had waited for more than an hour on a cold spring evening, before at last 'a foraging black-and-white snout came into view', and she stood 'in breathless excitement, feeling a sense of wonder I had not experienced for years'. From that moment she was hooked: over the next three years she spent more than a thousand hours observing badgers, sketching them and making notes about their behaviour – a consuming new passion that led first to the publication of her book *When Badgers Wake*, and later to the magnificent watercolours now published here.

Her own interest had been sparked off by reading the pioneer monograph on badgers by the leading authority, Dr Ernest Neal, published by Collins in their New Naturalist series during 1948. General knowledge of badgers was scanty at that time, and Eileen was quickly captivated by the elusive and mysterious nature of her new quarry. 'What is the lure of the badger,' she asked, 'that it keeps us out late at night in all weathers, cold and cramped, to wait for hours without moving?' She spent several years in the attempt to answer that question – but she emphasised how easy it was to start: 'Once we begin watching, there is no retreat, for the badger has a fascination few naturalists can resist;' and she added that 'to an artist his clean black-and-white head and the subtle curves of his body in movement are an immediate inspiration.'

Her main theatre of observation was an old marl-pit or dell extending to about half an acre – a lightly wooded hollow, with a steep cliff at one end, lying on its own amid fields – a place 'that might have been made for badgers'. To this lonely spot she would creep, evening after evening, sometimes with Eva or with a friend, but usually on her own, and the sheer physical endurance which she displayed was extraordinary. Frozen and soaked in winter,

Eileen's fascination with badgers grew into a full-scale passion.

Opposite:
Badger cub licking syrup from tree root

tormented by midges and mosquitoes in summer, stung by nettles, harassed by rats running over her feet, she ignored every discomfort in her search for fresh information and further insights. She would have been more comfortable if she had built a hide, but she made a point of doing without one, as she did not want to attract the attention of any other human by revealing that some special activity was in progress. The most she would do to rearrange nature was to sweep a path clear of leaves and twigs, so that she could make a silent approach, and to hack a small, level platform out of any steep slope on which she proposed to stand.

It is clear from her own accounts – modest as they are – that after a rudimentary start her field-craft reached a high standard. She learnt early on the paramount importance of approaching a sett into the wind, and stationing herself downwind of the holes from which she expected the badgers to emerge; and once she was in position, against the trunk of a tree, among the stems of an elder bush, or sitting on a stump, she would remain immobile for hours on end. When she fitted her torch with a red filter, she could use it without disturbing her quarry.

Her motives in making such efforts were mixed. Certainly she saw the badgers as an artistic challenge, to which she responded with her whole being; but she also wanted to study and stand up for a species which, in her view, the British persecuted with particular brutality. Her aim was to learn enough about badgers to make her own plea on behalf of their kind. In particular, she wanted to exonerate them from the charges of killing poultry and stealing eggs which farmers brought against them, and to help eradicate the horrible practice of gassing them in their setts.

So highly charged was the whole subject that she became secretive about her activities, and never divulged the whereabouts of the dell to anyone except trusted friends. (It was near Bull's Green, only a mile or so from Wildings; but from the hushed tones in which she spoke of it, it might have been fifty miles away.) She herself revelled in crepuscular or nocturnal expeditions: it suited her retiring nature to slip off on her own into the depths of the countryside, to become a creature of the dusk and dark, alone with the birds and animals that come to life at night – and the fascination of evening brought out the best in her writing:

> The sun is going down as the watch begins, and the stars come out slowly, faint points of light between the pattern of darkening leaves and twigs overhead. A late cuckoo calls; the blackbird, always an alarmist, begins his raucous '*Tchuch! Tchuch!*' that advertises his whereabouts to all within hearing, as he seeks out what he evidently feels will be an insecure resting place. At length he settles down, and all is quiet. A robin, the last bird to go to bed, twitters sleepily; the day closes. A rustle in the dry leaves tells where a woodmouse stirs, and presently he can be seen, a little, dark, intrepid figure against the sky, as he climbs the elder bush to melt into the leaves above.

As Eileen well knew, she cut a strange figure when setting out in the evening. After much experiment she settled on various well-tried combinations of clothes – often a skirt over tweed slacks tucked into boots, and a woollen coat on top of a mackintosh, all her garments being chosen for softness and silence: she rejected anything that made a noise when it brushed against twigs or branches in the wood. Although she rarely wore a hat, and never

went so far as to black her face, she did sometimes drape herself with foliage 'in the guise of a paratrooper, to good advantage'.

Just as she had gained the confidence of birds in her garden by existing quietly among them, so she won the trust of the badgers by allowing them to become used to her presence. After a while they accepted her completely, and one colony got to know her so well that they would follow her scent trail about in the hope that it would lead them to the peanuts which they associated with her.

It was not long before she achieved her dearest wish – to watch cubs at play – and long hours of observation enabled her to describe and draw scenes that few other naturalists had witnessed. No cubs born in captivity (she wrote) 'could have the clean and dapper appearance of these little creatures of the countryside. They were irresistible: perfect small editions of the adults . . .

They roll and tumble with one another, biting and snarling in mock battle; each very big in his own estimation ... When a badger-cub incites another to play, he fluffs his fur out at right angles to his body, making himself appear much bigger than his normal size. He then stands on stiff legs and bounces off the ground, to come down and make a rapid dart at his opponent ... Often in mid-air he will execute a curious little twist of his body, and his nose is brought round rapidly to his tail, and back. After several advances of this kind, the other cub usually responds, and the two are off in a game, the object of which seems to be to pin one's opponent down by the throat, and keep him there.

Tragedy blighted her second year of watching – 1952 – when a new colony she had found in a wood was gassed, leaving no survivors. But the inhabitants of the dell continued to flourish, and it was there, during her fourth summer, that she had her most magical experience. By luring that season's cubs with peanuts and syrup, she induced them to gather and play all round her, even to take food from her hands – a feat she claimed as unique. As she wrote, the touch of a cub's nose on her hand, or its tongue exploring her fingers, became 'a delightful and intimate part' of her watching. Then, on midsummer's night, as she set out for home across the fields, she suddenly found herself surrounded by an escort of little grey figures sweeping through the grass, as they circled round and round her on their way up to an old elm tree on a bank:

At last they drifted away, and I stood alone in the starlit silence. Perhaps the summer midnight had worked its charm on me, or it may be that badger-watchers, in company with bird-watchers, are not entirely human. I felt I had encountered a moment of rare good fortune, and that here, in company with those merry wanderers, I had met the fabulous spirit of midsummer night.

By the winter of 1953 she had collected enough notes and sketches to make the basis of a book, filled out by one digression on dormice and another on stoats, and in November she submitted it under the title *Badgers' Lure* to Macmillan, publishers of her children's stories. They, however, rejected it, as did both

Jonathan Cape and Collins; but James Fisher of Collins, in an appreciative letter, suggested that she should try the firm of Routledge & Kegan Paul. There her typescript – by now called *Merry Wanderers of the Night* – caught the interest of Colin Franklin, who, although only in his mid-twenties, was already a director of the company, and who, on 22 April 1954, wrote saying that even 'if the book does not hold together in its present form . . . I believe it could be recast in certain ways'. A week later he followed up with a letter of detailed suggestions, which Eileen, cautious as ever, sent to James Fisher, to see if he agreed with its recommendations. He did – and in the end the author accepted most of what Franklin had proposed. Taking his criticisms in good part, she reworked the text, incorporated the results of further research, changed the name of the book to *When Badgers Wake*, and sent in a new version of the typescript in June. This time Routledge accepted it, offering an advance of £50 against royalties.

As always, the author wished to keep a close eye on production, and laid out the pages herself, fitting the type round her numerous sketches; but everything went smoothly, and even she, with her demanding standards, was delighted with the appearance of the book when it came out in the autumn of 1955, with a complimentary preface by Dr Neal. 'It is giving me more pleasure than I have known for some time to have this book produced in such good taste, for the whole appearance is one of quality,' she wrote to Franklin. The dust-jacket was adorned, front and back, by a splendid drawing of badgers out in their snowy dell, with a full white moon hanging in the winter sky, and inside more than 150 of her sketches were handsomely reproduced.

Even after much expert attention from Franklin, the book remained unbalanced. The bulk of it consisted of four narrative sections, each describing one year's observations, with dissertations on dormice, stoats and birds sandwiched between. These, though attractive in themselves, had nothing to do with the main theme, and at the end the story simply petered out with the awful news that the colony had again been gassed. Here, if anywhere, was a chance for the author to release some bile or emotion, but she could not – or would not – let herself go in print, and ended her saga with the flat, wooden sentence: 'No badgers survived a final gassing on June 1.'

Yet any limitations in the text were more than redeemed by the

Opposite:
Badger cubs feeding on honey on a hawthorn tree

sketches. Here her upbringing as an artist came into its own. The drawings revealed her exceptional powers of absorbing detail instantaneously, of registering it in her mind and reproducing it faithfully. An expert naturalist like Ernest Neal immediately recognised the rightness of the attitudes caught by her pencil, and the way that the sketches accurately reflected animal behaviour, with their unique combination of liveliness and precision.

Reviews were excellent. 'Natural history as it should be written – and illustrated,' declared the *Times Educational Supplement*. The *Birmingham Post* particularly praised the sketches, which, it said, 'distilled the rhythm and quirks of wild badgers as no words could do'. In general, critics agreed that by the sheer persistence of her observation and the skill of her drawing the author had overcome her lack of training in the natural sciences and had made a valuable contribution to the knowledge of her subject. Dr Neal seconded this verdict, feeling that she had made some very perceptive first-hand observations, and that her work was greatly enriched by her attention to detail: small points, which most naturalists would have consigned to a footnote, often evoked full descriptions, and these made her text compelling. Routledge were sufficiently encouraged by early sales of the book to accept a second, which Eileen offered them in January 1956, again for an advance against royalties of £50.

So she began a new career, as an amateur naturalist-author. As an illustrator, she was in greater demand than ever – from Enid Blyton and other authors, from firms like the toymakers Kiddicraft, from the Central Council for Health Education, the National Association for Mental Health, manufacturers of stationery, and

many other companies; and she handled these diverse contacts with the speed and efficiency of a true professional. Yet her heart and imagination dwelt increasingly in the woods and fields, for her life had taken on a new pattern. She spent countless daylight hours, and almost as many nocturnal ones, going out in search of information, writing up her findings, and making sketches of what she had seen; and she symbolised the change by giving her home the name Wildings – that curious word meaning plants or trees growing wild.

At first she was worried that she might not have enough ideas for a second book, and in February 1956 she wrote to Franklin: 'Everything depends on my getting enough material in the coming year. I have some experiences to write on, and have been working on those, but I feel I must have more. It is vital to have first-hand experience.'

None of her readers could tell that this second volume of natural history, *Wild Encounters*, was written at a time of domestic crisis. For years her mother had been failing. As Blossom became more frail, Eileen and Eva first sat her in an armchair and made her knit squares; then they made her cut up newspapers, believing that by keeping her occupied they would somehow preserve her. Yet she descended into senility, and for several years a nurse came in daily to look after her; by the time she died at the age of seventy-three,

in April 1956, many of the letters the family received spoke in terms of a merciful release. 'It is a terrible loss, as we had always lived together, and we loved her very dearly,' wrote Eileen to Henry Greene. 'One feels so desolate.' Yet when the shock wore off it was no doubt a relief to both daughters that Blossom's sufferings were over; for by then they had no one to help them in the house and were finding domestic chores harder than ever, especially as Eva was becoming arthritic, and less able to do heavy jobs.

For her new book, Eileen fell back on her most fruitful source of all – her wild garden – and brought into use many episodes which had taken place in it over the past ten years. She also included a further year of badger observations, and disquisitions on foxes, hedgehogs and hares. *Wild Encounters* was more diverse than *When Badgers Wake*, but as soon as he read the new text in September 1956, Colin Franklin pronounced it 'better written, more carefully planned, and free from sentiment'. Eileen proposed a novel plan – that the whole book, type and drawings, should be printed in brown, which she felt would look 'less commercial than black'; but Franklin did not like the idea, and production went ahead with the aim of making the book look as much as possible like its predecessor.

Publication, in the autumn of 1957, was marred only by a dispute about the dust-jacket. Eileen was pleased by the appearance of the book itself, but the jacket appalled her. Her sketch of a blackcap in full song, perched in a wild rose bush, with a hare beneath, was printed in blue, pink and brown, but to her eye the colours were

'so thin that they practically disappear when one is a short distance from the book … I cannot understand how the printers have so completely ignored our request for deeper tones.' When Franklin reported that the printers were 'much grieved and upset by the whole matter', she replied tartly, 'I can assure you that any feelings the printers may have in this matter are nothing to my own disappointment. It is a long time since I felt so disheartened. It does not seem worthwhile putting so much effort into the work when a printer can step in and ruin it in this way.'

She need not have been so pessimistic. *Wild Encounters*, though less original in content than her first book, also received friendly reviews and sold reasonably well. It opened with an account of the author's garden and explained the close correlation between plants and birds; then it went on to describe bird life in detail, on and around the house – how wrens nested in the clematis on the pergola, how swallows brought up their young in the garage, and so on. Eileen's stance as an author was curiously uneven: for most of the time she wrote in the first person, and in lively enough fashion, but in some episodes she concealed her own identity behind fictitious characters like 'a gardener of my acquaintance', and told stories in such an elliptical way as to spoil their impact. The saga of throwing slugs over the garden boundary on to their neighbour's territory, which she had recounted so well to Henry Greene, lost all force with this treatment.

Even so, readers got a startling glimpse of the extent to which birds dominated the Soper household. If ever Eileen left the windows of her studio open and went out of the room, she wrote,

Birds nesting around the house

Top left: Robin in the shed
Top right: Communal wren roost
Above: Young swallows

she was likely to find 'nearly everything scattered on the floor' when she returned. The birds, knowing that she kept a tin of nuts in her desk, would ransack its surface the moment she went away, hurling pens, pencils, brushes, tubes of colour and sheets of paper to the floor. Most of the furniture in the house had been ruined by marauding great tits, which had once launched what she described as a 'crime wave':

> The arms of chairs and the corners of cushions were mutilated … Little bunches of horsehair poke through the covers, and feathers are frequently showing … My down quilt was also attacked … One day the tit got to work in earnest. The effect was of a miniature snowstorm. Down was scattered everywhere. It littered the bed, the surrounding furniture and the carpet, and the tit was still busy, pulling out more. The fascination was irresistible.

She also revealed that the house had been invaded by rare, yellow-necked field mice, one of which had severed the telephone flex, tried to chew its way into a drawer containing nuts, eaten a hole in the pocket of a coat and then retired to the spare room, where it made a nest, lined with lambswool taken from a snow-boot, in the middle of one of Eileen's skirts. Her response to these outrages was to acquire a cage-trap, and, when she had captured the marauder alive, to transport it to the middle of a field and release it. Even when the same clearly recognisable specimen was caught for the third time, she reacted only by driving it to a still more distant release-point.

Anyone reading *Wild Encounters* would have got the impression that the author lived deep in the heart of the country, and people who saw the garden at that time found it enthralling. Colin Franklin, who went to Wildings in the summer of 1957, wrote of the 'delightful and rare afternoon' he had spent there, and added that it was 'astonishing to see such a garden'. Among the plants he admired were George Soper's ferns, which had flourished mightily; and in August 1958 D. M. Campbell, Curator of the Royal Botanic Gardens at Kew, came down with a colleague to see them. He too much enjoyed his visit, described the collection of ferns as 'very fine', and took away for identification six other plants, which turned out to be two varieties of euonymus, one of syringa, one of campanula, one of viburnum and a large-leaf borage.

Yet even in her own sanctuary Eileen was beginning to feel threatened. 'Welwyn is utterly ruined with all the building-up,' she wrote to an old friend in the Cotswolds during January 1958, 'but we find it very difficult to move, as we have lived here all our lives. If ever you see a shack, barn or other building, or even a small spot of land going for a song, please do let me know. We pine for some little hut where we can go for a change sometimes, and where I can get material for my wildlife books. We have had it in mind for years, but such places are hard to find.'

Vexations came at her from every side: nearby owners sub-dividing their properties and building new houses in the gardens, cats invading, dogs barking, the Rural District Council proposing to desecrate Harmer Green Lane with lamp-posts. 'We feel that this urban introduction is not in keeping with the rural character of the lane, which we had hoped to retain,' she wrote in a stiff little note of protest. 'Already the wishes of the urban-minded members of the community have been fulfilled in many ways, against those of the older, country residents in the district.' To a troublesome neighbour, she set herself up as a long-suffering scientific researcher: 'I am sure your young son did not realise he was shooting a *tame* squirrel on Friday evening … This happened to be one of a tame pair whose activities I was watching closely, for the species is one which naturalists, including myself, are studying with a view to clearing up certain points in the ecology of these animals.'

Partial relief came when another neighbour, David Waterhouse, left his house Harmer Hyde, right next door to Wildings, and sold her a one-acre strip of his garden along her southern boundary, thus substantially increasing the size of the sanctuary (and incidentally bringing into the Sopers' hands a water garden, complete with artificial stream and pond, which their father had designed for his neighbour years before). Later, Eileen acted as spokeswoman for six other local residents in a joint preservation campaign, and, when they had won their point, sent them out bills of £1 each to meet the solicitor's fees incurred. Yet always a new threat loomed – and one of the worst was a plan by the Council to run a new sewer right through the middle of the garden. Against this horror, Eileen battled with admirable tenacity, writing to the Minister of Health and hinting in a letter to the drainage engineers retained by the Council that desecration of the sanctuary would force her to put in a very substantial claim for compensation:

We, and our father before us, have always maintained a bird sanctuary in the garden. In addition to this, many valuable plants are growing, which are irreplaceable. Any disturbance by excavating or digging we feel certain will drive away, never to return, various rare birds which, over a period of years, have gradually come to our preserve.

You will therefore see that if the sewer is put through the property, there will be a great deal of damage done, and we think that the compensation we should have to claim would be very high ... I would like to emphasise that my sister and I depend for our living on our work as naturalists and artists, and, in my own case, also as an author on these subjects. You will see from this that our business will be affected, and thus increase the claim ...

Even if the letter stretched the facts a little, it had an excellent effect, and Eileen sustained her campaign against the new sewer so strongly that in the end it bypassed her property altogether, leaving Wildings on its own septic tank.

The idea of moving, or just of taking a holiday cottage, flickered on and off for the next ten years: At one moment Eileen sent for particulars of a building known as the Old Granary at Orford, in Suffolk, advertised as 'suitable for conversion to a private dwelling-house', and going for £850. Later she considered a house in the village of Amberley, in Sussex – a county to which her father had thought of moving before the war, and one for which she retained a special affection. 'We are always longing for Sussex,' she told one friend. 'It used to be our favourite county for holidays and sketching.' More and more she was oppressed by the feeling that

Hertfordshire had been over-run by houses and people. 'One needs to live about 200 miles from London to get any peace,' she wrote. Yet all ideas of moving were no more than dreams, for she could never face the ordeal of pulling up the roots that her father had put down so long ago. The idea of leaving the house, in which she had spent fifty years, was bad enough, but to have abandoned the garden, and all the wild creatures in it, would surely have killed her.

Far from making serious plans to move, the sisters were still doing their utmost to preserve and enhance the sanctuary. When they took possession of their new strip of territory Eileen welcomed it keenly as fresh habitat for birds: 'I viewed the fine grass under the pine plantation as a possible nesting-site for willow-warblers, and the trees as supports for nesting boxes.' Yet it was the old water garden that held the greatest possibilities, and soon she found herself on hands and knees, alongside Eva, chipping away with hammer and chisel to enlarge the cracks in the floor of the old pond so that they could be sealed with fresh cement. After prodigious labours, their efforts were rewarded by the sight of water tumbling again over the little cascades, and birds bathing once more in the various pools. The new garden delighted Eileen, not least because it attracted creatures like newts and water boatmen, and also enabled her to grow aquatic plants such as lilies, hostas and bog bean.

The few visitors who did penetrate Wildings' defences were all struck by Eileen's devotion to her father – an undying love which constantly surfaced in reference to his work, to the landscape he had painted, and to the experiences she had shared with him, the un-named subject of her poem:

How well he loved these things
  Who now no more shall know
The gentle touch of rain,
  The glory of the snow.

How well he loved to walk
  Beside the leisured plough
Watching the brown surf break
  As from an old ship's prow,
And on his mind would take
  All colour, form and tone,
To hold as captive there
  The vision for his own.
And as he watched the team,
  The muscles' pull and strain
Traced by the highlights' flow,
  The long, looped line of rein,
  The harness, the lifting mane,
All on his sight were wrought
  That he, inspired, might bring
Life to the empty page:
  Imprisoned beauty sing
To a less comely age.

Eight

IN THE INTERVALS of gardening, Eileen had begun an important new line of artistic activity. Of all the animals she had studied, badgers were her firm favourites: every aspect of their behaviour fascinated her, but she loved above all the fact that they were nocturnal. While she was watching them, she became a creature of the night, bewitched by the moon. *Wild Encounters* included a lyrical passage describing how, at 2.30 one morning, the badgers had gone back into their sett, leaving her alone:

> I was left in contemplation of the shadows. As I listened to the absolute silence, I heard a faint hush creep over the fields, a sound that was hardly perceptible, yet defining the change from night to day. With it, a white mist enveloped the country-side, and I watched the shadows gradually fade. The moon, which a few moments before had been almost dazzling in its brilliance, became a dull amber sphere through the thickening curtain of mist. The dawn broke.

Now, to Colin Franklin, she wrote: 'I have been doing some colour work of the badgers, both cubs and adults, and I wonder whether you would feel it could be a practical proposition to produce a book with a limited number of these watercolour studies.' Her idea was that the book might serve as a gift folio of drawings, which could be detached and framed. 'There are no colour pictures of badgers on the market,' she added, 'and I do feel that, with the popularity the badger now receives, the idea has possibilities.'

The notion proved stillborn, largely because a book on the lines she suggested would have been ruinously expensive to produce. Eileen, however, began to paint with new inspiration. There, in her

north-facing studio, plagued by birds in summer, frozen in winter, she worked as she had never worked before. Because she rarely dated her pictures, it is no longer clear exactly when most of them were completed; but it can safely be said that all the watercolours in this book came from that inspired period of ten years or so beginning in 1957, and that all of them were taken from life, based on scenes the artist herself had witnessed, and reconstructed from sketches made on the ground. She painted them not for commercial gain, but for the sheer joy and satisfaction that painting gave her.

In the badger pictures, winter predominates. Again and again a white and frosty full moon beams down through bare branches into the dell where the badgers are playing, reflecting the artist's passion for nocturnal expeditions. A critic might say that the animals are a shade anthropomorphic, and that the badgers, with their slightly dished faces, look more charming than they should. It could be maintained that if Eileen had gone through the rigorous discipline of art school, she might have seen her quarry in a rather more analytical light: her paintings might have been still more realistic, and she might have avoided a tendency to prettify her subjects, especially foxes. But nobody can deny the strength and balance of her compositions, their intense atmosphere, or the wealth of behavioural detail that they illustrate. Experts find it hard to compare these pictures with those of other wildlife artists, for they are not in the least derivative, but thoroughly original.

Once again, her industry was astonishing. Purely from the number of works she produced, one can deduce that on average she must have completed one painting every fortnight – and this in the middle of innumerable other commitments. She also drew an enormous amount, often rejecting ten or a dozen fully worked versions of the same subject before she was satisfied.

It was characteristic of her to tell hardly anyone what she was doing. She kept the door of the studio locked, and rarely let a visitor see inside. When Colin Franklin came down she did let him see some of her father's etchings, but that was extremely unusual: most visitors got no farther than the garden or the parlour next to the kitchen. Eileen's protective instincts extended not only to her own work but to her father's as well; and if she was reluctant to let any outsider see the family's pictures, still less was she willing to part with any of them. For years Marguerite Roe had begged her to sell some small drawing or print. There was no question of

cadging one as a gift: she made it clear from the start that she would pay. But Eileen always brushed the request aside with some excuse, and never let her have anything. Occasionally a dealer called at the house hoping to secure prints or paintings by her father, but always he was quickly despatched, often by a sharp call from an upstairs window.

Slowly but surely Eileen's habits were becoming stranger. She had, for instance, evolved a singular method of making tea. Because tea came from India, it was dangerous stuff – for everyone knew what Indians did with their hands; and so it needed firm treatment before it became fit to drink. She would therefore boil a kettle, pour the water on to the tealeaves in a metal pot, and then boil that for twenty minutes, to make sure all germs were exterminated. The resulting stew of course tasted disgusting, but the sisters would drink no other, and if ever they went to call at any house where there was a chance of being offered a cup of tea, they would take their own with them in a Thermos flask.

Fear of catching something meant that they could never eat out, and Eileen became adept at making excuses to cover their need to stay at home. When Colin Franklin invited her and Eva to dinner, her reply was typically evasive. 'We would have enjoyed this tremendously,' she wrote, 'but I am in some difficulty, as I am not feeling very fit: nothing serious, but it complicates life, and I have to be bothered with diet. All very inconvenient. I hope you will forgive me.' Little did Franklin know that the sisters boiled the clothes pegs with which they hung out washing to dry, that if any garment fell to the ground outdoors they boiled it within inches of disintegration, and that when they took delivery of a new bath they washed it down with Dettol 'in the interests of hygiene . . . as it had been handled by a number of people on the way' – after which Eileen had the nerve to complain to the manufacturers that her treatment had stained the side-panel. And of course, in the midst of this frenzied persecution of germs, they gladly allowed their house to be over-run by birds and mice.

Eileen had become acutely sensitive about her appearance, and refused to pose in front of a camera. 'I am afraid I cannot comply,' she told a photographer who asked if he might do a publicity article about her. 'I am so ill at ease with a camera that I never consent to being photographed.' When publication of one of her books was imminent, and the *Welwyn & Hatfield Advertiser* proposed to send

Eileen A. Soper

out a reporter to interview her, she wrote in some agitation to the Editor: 'I am very sorry to find, on looking into my diary, that it is not possible to give an interview to your reporter ... You may remember that I do not like reference to one's age in newspapers, and I shall be grateful if you will kindly respect my wishes in this matter.[She was then in her early fifties.] I will be glad also if you can avoid giving my full address. I find this brings too many callers!'

In matters of diet, the sisters had grown extremely conservative. Connoisseurs of potatoes, they could distinguish one variety from another by the taste, and usually would eat one kind only – Golden Wonder, for which they ordered seed from Messrs Alexander & Brown of Perth, and which they had grown for them by a local farmer, who was forbidden to use artificial fertiliser or chemical sprays. Another staple of the Sopers' diet was peas, which they grew themselves – and great was their dudgeon when, for three years running, their crop failed. When Eileen sent specimens to the Hertfordshire Institute of Agriculture for analysis, the answer came back that the plants were infected with a fungus disease known as Fusarium root rot, and that the only way of eradicating it was to grow peas on fresh ground.

Trapped as they were at Wildings, the sisters did most of their shopping by post, and Eileen was constantly sending off esoteric requests – for special pencils, paper, a cocoa mat 30 × 36 inches to fit a well one inch deep, two pairs of crêpe nylon stockings (No. H 10, size: small), particulars of infra-red equipment for night viewing, a Longworth small mammal live-capture trap, patterns of 'any washing material with which I could make a blouse to wear with the enclosed tweed'. In clothes, as in furnishings, her favourite colour was a soft blue, like that of speedwell: garments, carpets, curtains all tended to be the same.

Between her painting and illustrating, Eileen kept up her wildlife observation and writing. In the autumn of 1958 she completed a third book, which, after some edgy debate, was called *Wanderers of the Field*. She herself did not like the title, and suggested others, among them *Youth in Winter*, and when Routledge held out against them, she gave in with ill grace. Characteristically, she made two drafts of her reply to Colin Franklin in which she capitulated. In the first she wrote, 'I think *Wanderers of the Field* is very dull and will be passed over. A number of those I suggested were in my opinion better, being more unusual and arresting.' But in the event she scrapped this letter and simply wrote: 'I have entered the title [in the proofs] though it is not what I would have liked.'

Her dissatisfaction extended both to the jacket and to the finished book, which she saw in November 1959. 'On the whole it is quite pleasing,' she wrote of the jacket, 'but how much better it would have been for a little more life in the blue and the glow from the sun.' For the production of the book itself, she had little but damnation:

In parts it is, I suppose, quite pleasing, and here and there the reproductions are fair, but I expected something much better … In general the illustrations are thick and smudgy. Some of the plates are truly dreadful … What have they done to get that horrible bother of tone all over the work? And why, after all my trouble to see that the drawings were correctly set up in the paste-up, do they move the swan drawing and put it askew? Words fail me.

Young tawny owl

Franklin replied soothingly, and managed to preserve his friendly relationship with the author; but perhaps her irritation stemmed from the fact that the new book lacked the impact of its predecessors. It was very much the mixture as before, and concerned birds, badgers, mice, voles and squirrels, with the accent on youth and the start of life: adequate, agreeable natural history, but not much more. Sales of the book reflected this falling-off in originality. By the end of 1960 *When Badgers Wake* had sold 2700 copies, *Wild Encounters* 2000, and *Wanderers of the Field* only 1400. In all, Eileen earned no more than £650 from the three books put together – a miserable return for the huge amount of work done in observation, note-taking, sketching, writing and drawing spread over the past ten years.

Even so, she was horrified to learn, in 1963, that Routledge, finding themselves left with a large stock of all three titles, were about to offer them at half-price in a National Book League sale. 'This is a severe blow,' she wrote to Franklin. 'I can think of few things more damaging to an author's reputation.' His reply was that a sale of that kind never damaged anyone's reputation – but she could never accept with equanimity any departure from what she took to be the highest standards. Thus when Brockhaus bought the German rights in *When Badgers Wake*, she was appalled to find that they were intending to bring out a cheap-format edition; but her guns were spiked when the firm courteously offered her the chance to check their German translation, and she was forced to pass it up because she could not read the language. It was a measure of the smallness of her world that she did not think of getting some friend to look at the German for her.

Nine

THE YEAR 1961 brought two important newcomers to Wildings: the first was the celebrated bird photographer Eric Hosking, and the second, muntjac, or barking deer.

Word had spread that the birds in Eileen's garden were the tamest anyone had ever seen, and Hosking conceived the idea of photographing them as they fed from her hand, partly for his own collection, partly to get pictures for advertising Swoop bird food. When he wrote to say that he hoped to come out from his home in North London at the end of January, Eileen replied, 'I think I should warn you that a bright day is essential, as I would not like to use a flash. It might spoil the birds' tameness, which seems unique.'

In her first draft of the letter she added: 'If you feel it is worth battling with all the difficulties to add the Soper tits to your records, we shall be very pleased to see you'; but even she, innocent as she was, seems to have realised that the sentence was not altogether appropriate, and in her final version she changed it to: 'If this is not too great a handicap, we shall be very pleased for you to add some of our tits to your records.'

Hosking – an ebullient little Cockney, whose whole life was devoted to birds – went down on 30 January, and received a warm welcome. He was in the end obliged to use a flash, but it seemed to upset the birds very little. Eileen was greatly excited by the project, which she regarded as 'all very hush-hush'; and after two further visits, and an exchange of gifts, the parties were addressing each other by their Christian names, and a lifelong friendship had begun. 'Dear Eric,' wrote Eileen on 14 February,

These are exquisite! I hope you are as thrilled as I am with the results. What a vast number of successes! The birds never seem

to have taken up the exact position twice, and you have caught so many and varied a collection of poses and compositions ... The nuthatch has come out beautifully. I am delighted with the one where he is in the foreground with a coal tit ... I hope he will come to hand for the pictures next time ... We will look forward to seeing you on Friday, weather permitting. Meanwhile, I will do my best to put in some intensive training. Nutty is here at the studio window again as I am writing, and a robin has come in and is hopping round my feet, also tits overhead!

Another batch of pictures again sent Eileen into raptures: 'These are splendid! There are some wonderful pictures among them. We are both truly delighted.' So thrilled was she that she sent Eric a painting of long-tailed tits, which he declared to be 'quite delightful', and torrents of ornithological news began to pour out of Harmer Green. In mid-March, when a cold spell set in, she reported that 'quite a crowd of birds came to the tray and to my hand ... I put up the hazel pole with the hole on top and baited it with some of your cheese. It seems rather cruel to tell you this, but at

mid-morning a great spotted woodpecker came up the pole and took some cheese from the top! Just the spot on where your camera was focussed yesterday.'

Nuthatch in the garden

During the summer Hosking arranged that *Country Life* should publish an illustrated article about the Soper birds, and he generously presented Eileen with half the fee of thirty guineas he received for the use of his photographs – one of a number of kind gestures he made towards her over the next few years. Always he wrote to her with news of his extensive trips abroad, and at Christmas both parties would exchange cards and calendars of their own design.

The other newcomer of 1961 – the muntjac – also had a lasting

influence on Eileen's life. Muntjac, or barking deer, which stand only about twenty inches tall at the shoulder, had originally been imported to England from the Far East by the eleventh Duke of Bedford, who installed a breeding group in his park at Woburn Abbey at the turn of the century. In due course they escaped and began to spread through the south of England: being non-gregarious, and living in family groups, they tended to colonise a wood and then, when the population became uncomfortably high, to move on, in a kind of creeping takeover.

Eileen had already sought them out in some of her outlying beats, but great was her delight when, one February morning, she walked down the garden and checked the mud for tracks of nocturnal visitors. Expecting at most to see traces of a fox or hare, she was amazed to find the slots of a muntjac doe and fawn. Since, in her view, 'deer bring a sense of charm to any place they haunt', she was immensely excited, and felt that in attracting so large a mammal the garden had achieved a new dimension. Thereafter she pursued and watched the little deer on her own territory with the single-minded enthusiasm that she had lavished on the badgers in the dell.

It was the harsh winter of 1962–3 that gave her the chance to get to know them well. The first snow fell on December 11, and although that lot cleared, a blizzard at Christmas laid a frozen mantle over the land for the next five weeks. In purely aesthetic terms Eileen found it exhilarating:

Snow brings a breadth and simplicity to the landscape which does much to obliterate the scars of modern development. For me it has an irresistible lure ... It is a rare experience to be in the field before human footfall has shattered the wide expanse: the silence, the clear air, the sense of remoteness are compelling.

Yet on a practical level she dreaded the cold, because it inflicted so much suffering on birds and wild animals. As she reported, 'On the first bitter winds countless birds flocked to the garden in search of food' – greenfinches, redwings, fieldfares and tits innumerable, and she laboured heroically to feed and save as many as she could. 'Half my day goes in preparing food for them,' she told Eric, 'putting it out and breaking the ice on the ponds ... The hungry hoards are enormous, and we cannot keep them satisfied.'

That winter, for the first time, she also made special efforts on behalf of the deer. Over Christmas she set to work in one of the garden thickets to build a shelter 'from stakes reinforced with peasticks', which she thatched with a thick layer of bracken, 'making it more or less wind and weather proof'. A dry bed of hay 'added to indoor comfort', and over the next few days slots leading in and out showed that 'the shelter had been discovered and was already in use'.

Eileen's guest was a buck muntjac, which began to take the apples and brown bread that she put out, and gradually grew more tolerant of the humans who kept coming in search of him: whenever they inadvertently met him face-to-face, he would break cover and move off, though not very fast or very far:

> As trespassers in our own garden we crept about, furtively peering into thickets as we passed, anxious not to disturb him if it could be avoided, though he rarely showed panic, and took to his feet reluctantly, to walk away and stand watching the intruders before wandering again into cover.

Eileen's aim, as always, was to observe and sketch, and she was pleased that, when the thaw came, the buck continued to live in the garden. In the spring, once the growth of leaves had made watching more difficult, she wrote off to a London gunsmith for a roe-deer call – an instrument which she hated in principle, since it had been designed for hunters – and one evening ensconced herself in some brushwood at the base of an elm tree, to see if her new device would work:

The sound that came forth was unlike any I had heard made by muntjac, but, to my surprise, almost at once the buck answered. I replied on the whistle, and he barked again. I heard the patter of his hoofs as he came towards me, and again I repeated the call. He moved nearer, and I could then see him as he stood below the bank where I was hidden: his head up, ears forward, listening intently. But he was too close for further experiment, which would almost certainly have given me away.

So began a period of surveillance, sketching and learning about deer, which Eileen kept up for nearly eight years. Gradually she increased the number of shelters to seven, and night after night she sat out, binoculars at the ready, in the little summerhouse that stood in the wooded part of the garden, waiting for the buck to come and feed on the apples and other delicacies that she had put out to lure him. What she spent on bait is anybody's guess. Once the buck had shown a preference for Cox's Orange Pippins, he got no other apples, except sometimes Bramley's, and these had to be sprinkled with sugar to make them more palatable. The muntjac also put away huge quantities of Spanish chestnuts, which she bought in twelve-pound bags. Closer to the house there was a memorable confrontation between the buck and a hedgehog, another regular recipient of Eileen's bounty. One evening the hedgehog was already dining off cheese when the deer came out and began to eat apples, without apparently noticing that it had a companion: then, suddenly realising that it was not alone, the muntjac leapt in the air and landed almost astride the hedgehog, which scuttled away, 'tumbling over itself with anxiety' – an episode which Eileen captured in some beautiful action-sketches.

She herself might have found it difficult to analyse her motives in devoting so much time to the deer: she wanted to learn all she could about their behaviour, of course, but she was driven also by the magical attraction of coming close to a wild creature, in all senses of the phrase. Recording how, when she surprised the buck, he would retreat only a short distance and then stand at gaze, watching her, she remarked: 'This I concluded was as near to friendship as I was ever likely to get.'

In due course a doe appeared in the garden, and then, one April, a tiny spotted fawn. When another fawn only two or three weeks old appeared the following January, Eileen realised that muntjac did indeed breed all the year round, as she had heard rumoured. Then came another young buck, 'slim and golden', whom she called Adonis. Even though she did not favour the use of names with inevitable human associations, she started to label them all, for ease of reference: Little Fella, Tiny, Freckles, Darky, Tim. There was one awful disaster when roving dogs savaged and killed Little Fella, but the remaining deer soon settled down again and continued to use the garden as their sanctuary.

Ten

OBSESSED THOUGH SHE WAS by the deer, she had also to carry on with the rest of her life. In January 1963, after twenty-seven years, her beloved Riley finally reached the end of its road. In the last week of November she went out to collect bracken for her muntjac shelters, 'and filled the car with it', but then the engine 'more or less packed up' and a mechanic thought that two of the valves had blown. She already had on order a new Hillman Minx, but the prospect of it seemed very dull, and she could hardly bear to see the old car go. 'You would have laughed to see me trying to take photos of her on Monday morning before the garage took her away,' she told Eric. 'Ridiculously sentimental, I suppose, but I have had her so long.'

In February she made her one and only television appearance in the BBC's 'Animal Magic' series. She was filmed briefly luring a bird to feed on her hand and sketching birds beside an open window outside which a constant stream of subjects presented themselves on a table loaded with tit-bits. The programme attracted widespread attention, not least from a ten-year-old schoolboy, Stephen Roberts, who wrote from South Wales saying, 'Please send me a letter on how to make them come on my hand.' In its thoroughness, its politeness, and its direct way of addressing a child, Eileen's answer was absolutely characteristic:

Dear Stephen,

Thankyou for your letter. I am glad to hear that you enjoyed the television programme. You will have to be very patient to get the birds to come to your hand. You must wait a long time with your hand out of the window and offer them something they like very much. The tits especially like broken peanuts, and robins love grated cheese. If they are very shy, hide

yourself partly behind the curtain till they have learned to come to your hand, then you can gradually show more of yourself. I think if you can be patient and quiet they will trust you after a while. You must never make sudden movement or noise, because birds are very timid and sensitive.

I hope you will always be interested in birds and try to help them by encouraging other boys to like them also, and never to take their eggs or destroy their nests.

With every wish for your successful bird watching and feeding.

Yours sincerely,
Eileen A. Soper.

Of the many young people inspired by her example, none was more strongly influenced than John Lister-Kaye, who in 1963 was still at Allhallows School, in Dorset, where he had already shown a passionate interest in natural history, and in particular had

reared a weasel called Wilba, which spent much time in his pockets. Having obtained an introduction to Eileen, he was brought over to lunch at Wildings by his father, Sir John Lister-Kaye, Bt, – and he never forgot his day in that extraordinary garden: as he described it, the most astonishing introduction to natural history that a schoolboy could possibly have had. Later, he remembered Eileen as fairly unkempt, with holes in the elbows of her cardigan, and her hair, now grey, carelessly twisted into a bun. Luckily she took an immediate fancy to Wilba, who ran up the sleeve of her smock and out at the neck; she also took a shine to Sir John, so things went well from the start.

When a grey squirrel came in through the open window to join them at lunch, and dormice kept popping out of the sofa, the visitors could scarcely believe their eyes. Afterwards, as the rest of them talked, Eva rapidly modelled a bird in clay. When they walked down the garden, young John was amazed to see birds fly down and settle on Eileen's head, as she fed them with crumbs of cheese from the wide pocket of her smock, and a muntjac come out to take a biscuit from her hand. Eileen suggested that he should write, and she should illustrate, an article about Wilba for the quarterly journal, the *Countryman*, and this duly appeared the following year; afterwards, John joined her on numerous badger-watching forays and became a firm friend. But the long-term effect which that first day had on the boy was incalculable, for it set him on course to become a full-time naturalist, and proved a stepping-stone to a distinguished career in wildlife management and conservation.

In trying to help young men of promise, Eileen was always sympathetic and encouraging. She could, on the other hand, be thoroughly acerbic with people who irritated her. In November 1964 she was glad to receive a letter, addressed to 'Miss I. Soper', informing her that she and Eva had each been left £100 by a recently deceased aunt; but, perhaps roused by the scarcely credible name of the solicitors who handled the legacy, Messrs Meneer Idle & Bracket, and by the illiteracy of their communication, she sent back a whiplash of an answer:

I and my sister Miss Eva L. Soper are both nieces and live at the above. But we presume you are addressing me, as my Christian name is Eileen, pronounced of course Ileen, which

Opposite: Early summer roses

appears to have caused your mistake in the initial. One other small point: Welwyn is spelt thus, not Welling, as in your letter.

Eileen's contact with the BBC brought new friends, in the form of Jeffery Boswall, Producer for the Natural History Unit, and Winwood Reade, Producer of the 'Animal Magic' series, with both of whom she maintained contact for years. She also contributed drawings to several more 'Animal Magic' programmes, but never again herself appeared on the screen.

During the summer of 1966 the house was thrown into chaos by the need to renew all the electrical wiring. This major renovation was essential, as there had been a bad short-circuit in the winter, and two wires had been found fused together. But, as Eileen reported to Eric, she 'nearly went crazy' as the workmen proceeded from room to room, tearing up the floors and ripping old cables from the walls:

> I spent ages packing up all Dad's work, crating an incredible amount and endeavouring to find somewhere safe to put things. The old air-raid shelter was the only place the men didn't invade. Now that they have gone, the difficulty is to try to mend the house, as they have wrecked the floors and walls everywhere. At the moment I have about a yard round my desk; which I can just reach. The rest of the room needs a helicopter approach, and we have lost so many things in the packing-up. My difficulty is to sort and destroy wherever possible the vast amount of material that has accumulated over the years.

That was her difficulty, in a nutshell. Try as she might, she found it almost impossible to throw anything away, and the house continued to silt up with papers and possessions – not just the studio, but the kiln-room and sitting-room as well. Outside, the garden began slowly but inexorably to grow out of control. Already the sisters had lost the services of Harold, who had been forced to retire by poor health, and now they depended on the sporadic efforts of Bertie Bland for help with the heavy jobs like digging which they themselves could not manage. The gradual deterioration – barely noticeable in its early stages – did not much

worry Eileen at first, for more cover and extra wildness made the sanctuary still more comfortable for deer.

During the winter of 1966 the sisters had an unnerving nocturnal visitation, which Eileen described vividly in a letter to Eric. As usual, they had left on the outside light on the pergola, so that they could watch any deer that came to feed below the terrace:

We are 'as well as can be expected' after our adventures with a burglar. I went to the bedroom window one night to look out for deer and saw a man with an iron bar looking into the downstairs room where Eva was sitting. Needless to say, we dialled 999. Half the county police were here in about ten minutes, though it seemed like hours. Meanwhile Eva had a view of him looking in the window again from her lookout upstairs. We stayed in the locked bedroom, and he came in downstairs before the police arrived. This alarmed him, and he fled, but was caught by a Bobby who vaulted the gates and caught up with him as he started his car in the road.

Various tits feeding from the hand

Below:
Great tits' threat display

This version of the story differed slightly from one she told to Marguerite Roe. In that account, she herself was in the downstairs room when she first saw the burglar outside the window, on the verandah. With great presence of mind, and no mean courage, she stifled her instinct to dash for the telephone: yawning and stretching ostentatiously, as if about to go up to bed, she crossed the room slowly and accelerated only when she was out of sight, at the bottom of the staircase. Either way, she behaved most creditably. What alarmed her more than the actual visit of the burglar was the thought that she and Eva would have to attend the judicial court, to give evidence at his trial. Any appearance in a public building was, in Eileen's words, a 'horrifying ordeal' – but for reasons which only she and Eva could explain.

Perhaps it was the effort of sorting and packing her father's pictures that prompted her to offer *Country Life* an illustrated article about his wood engravings. This appeared in the issue of 2 February 1967, and turned out a rather dull piece, clumsily shaped and poorly edited (it nowhere said, for instance, when George Soper had been born, when he had died, when and where he had worked, or where he had lived). Even so, there came through it a powerful nostalgia for the days of farming before mechanisation: the four engravings reproduced on the two-page spread made a strong impact, and the appearance of the article brought letters from far and wide, mostly from people wanting to know how they could acquire Soper prints.

The answer, in a phrase, was that they could not. In defending her father's reputation and assets, Eileen was always extraordinarily protective; and now, even though she had several hundred prints of his engravings, and more than a thousand of his etchings, she told almost every correspondent that prints were impossible to find. Given the publicity created by her own article, she could have made a lot of money by judicious sales; instead, the most she would allow was that 'there are a few proofs of some of his etchings and drypoints'. Given time, she said, she might be able to look out one or two of these – and in the end she did sell a few at five guineas apiece. To one inquirer she hinted mysteriously, 'Later I hope to have some drawings and water colours available', but she offered no explanation as to where these pictures might come from, and she several times repeated that no prints of the engravings existed. Nor would she allow the Country Landowners'

Association to proceed with a plan to enlarge one of the etchings, which they wanted to hang in their pavilion at that year's Royal Show. 'I am sorry not to be able to grant your request,' she wrote, 'but I know my father would not have consented to the enlargement. The aim of his wood engraving was to achieve quality, and I do not feel it is suitable for such enlargement.' Her instinct was evidently to keep a tight hold of everything he had left – and the same applied to her own pictures, even to copies of her books. When Alison Boardman, who had sat for her as a child, asked for a copy of her favourite *Happy Rabbit*, she replied that she had none – even though she was sitting on a whole pile of them. To several correspondents she suggested that she might one day bring out a book of her father's work – and the idea seems to have grown on her during that summer, for in July she wrote to the Royal Society of Painter Etchers and Engravers, saying that she had 'for some time' been planning to publish her father's engravings in book form, and asking them to suggest a fine-art publisher. The Society promptly recommended Charles Skilton, but for the moment Eileen let the matter drop.

Crowds of hungry birds in winter snow

As for her own pictures: every summer she sent four or five to the annual exhibition held in London by the Society of Wildlife Artists, of which she had become a founder-member in 1964. But quite apart from the few she sold there she was piling up a substantial number of watercolours in the studio, and she seems never to have thought of holding an exhibition of her own. Over her illustration work, and indeed over her own books, she was uninhibitedly commercial, exacting every penny she could from publishers; but with her paintings she was much less aggressive. It was as if her illustrations came from her head, and counted for little, but her paintings, which came from the heart, were too precious to be disposed of.

For someone permanently worried about money she was curiously passive in this respect. Her letters complained more and more about the expense of things, of the difficulty of making ends meet: in 1967 she had sold the family pianola, and tried, but failed, to sell the pottery kiln. Yet she was still earning a good income, she had no dependants (human, at any rate) and no mortgage or loans on which she had to make payments. Besides, she and Eva between them had built up a sizeable amount of capital, which was producing income of its own and growing all the time. Although in

fact not hard up at all, Eileen seems to have suffered from the quintessentially Edwardian malaise of fearing that if she spent a shilling of her capital it would inevitably mean ruin.

In 1966 Routledge published the Eileen Soper Wildlife Series – three illustrated pamphlets of sixty-eight pages each, entitled *New Tracks*, *From Nesting into Flight* and *Well-worn Paths*. Designed for children, these were in fact a regurgitation of material from *Wanderers of the Field*, and were said by the publishers to have been brought out in response to many requests from teachers in primary and junior schools, who had found the book ideal for children. But her main literary project during the 1960s was her new book *Muntjac*, which she finished in the summer of 1968. As with her work on badgers, she was secretive about her dealings with deer, and before she submitted the typescript to a publisher, she sought the advice of Ernest Neal:

> I am in a quandary to know what to do. I am hoping to publish my book on muntjac, but now that it has come to contacting a publisher, I wonder how I can safeguard my findings from the unscrupulous! One's typescript goes out to a reader, who at once has before him all one's discoveries, so to speak. I have found out the length of the gestation-period of muntjac, and watched a buck re-growing the antlers from casting almost to

cleaning date, and added to [understanding of] the vocabulary of the deer, and many close observations have given me insight into behaviour. As very little has been so far recorded about muntjac, all this might be of sufficient interest to be used by a reader: he might even be working for a national newspaper on a weekly nature note. Who knows, one might find all one's secret (!) information made public before the book comes into print.

Neal replied soothingly, and Eileen mastered her suspicions sufficiently to submit the typescript to Routledge, who had brought out three of her earlier books. They, however, dithered over it for so long that she tried it on Longmans, who accepted it, and published it in November 1969 – but not before there had been a characteristic explosion from the author. She had drawn a plan of the garden, to be used as the book's endpapers, but then was outraged to find that someone at Longmans had decided to improve it, without consulting her. 'I have just received from the printers the first half of the page-proofs,' she wrote, 'and find to my astonishment that the map for the endpapers has been entirely redrawn. This I cannot tolerate on any account, and there is, at this late hour, only one solution – to delete the map from the book.' In a second letter three days later, she let fly again:

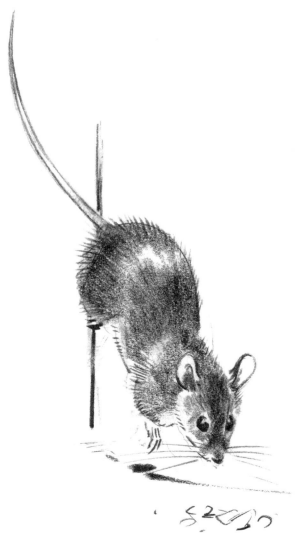

Your artist has attempted, in his pictorial version, to show what he assumes is the entire detailed landscape. This is of course impossible without knowing the area and making sketches on the spot. The result is that he has failed entirely to convey the truly wild environment to which the deer have been attracted. They would not have established themselves as they have, had the garden been of the open and formal type which this map depicts.

The book appeared without the map. Like her other works of natural history, it was primarily a narrative of observations and events, and established many useful points; but in the course of it the author also sometimes became unusually polemical, for instance launching an attack on the practice of catching animals and fitting them with radios or other markers for the purpose of tracking their movements. This attracted the enmity of Dr Oliver Dansie, a

general practitioner who lived close by and had himself done much work catching muntjac and equipping them with ear-tags, collars and radios in attempts to establish their territorial habits. In a blistering review of Eileen's book, Dansie dismissed it as amateurish and incompetent, thereby opening a rift that never healed. Altogether, Eileen's relations with other deer-fanciers were uneasy: although she received a good deal of help from members of the British Deer Society, she declined several invitations to join it, preferring always to retain her independence.

By the time that *Muntjac* came out, its subjects had established a paralysing domination over the author. Just as birds had often tyrannised the Soper household in the past, so now the deer imposed severe restrictions on human use of the garden. Once they had taken to feeding near the front of the house, everything had to be organised so as to minimise disturbance. Eileen kept the garden gate bolted, and posted on it a note directing callers to the back door. She asked friends not to telephone after dark unless the call was urgent, 'as the bell frightened and bewildered all but the most tolerant of the deer'. She herself became reluctant to take her car out in the evening, and she fiercely resented the 'unnecessary engine-revving and slamming of doors' indulged in by other drivers. Warning regular visitors not to come round after dark, she tried

to make all tradesmen call during daylight hours; and in order to cut down the number of their visits, she ordered her animal food in large consignments – only to find that field-mice, voles and even shrews ate their way into the packages stored outside in sheds.

As she herself admitted, her own freedom of action was much restricted: 'No work could be done or bonfires lit where deer were likely to be harbouring in adjacent thickets. Scything was banned in the wild garden, as it deprived the deer of cover. Consequently stinging nettles and other invasive weeds grew to rampant proportions, casting their seed far and wide.'

In other words, the muntjac powerfully reinforced the reclusive habits of their human mentor, and gave her yet another excuse for closing the barriers of her secret garden against the outside world. It was symptomatic of her isolation that she ignored the seasonal time-changes prescribed for the rest of the nation, and kept her clocks the same, summer and winter. Friends were distressed to see how suspicious she and Eva had become of almost everybody: they seemed to assume that people were automatically against them, and would take advantage of them if they relaxed their vigilance or lowered their defence. In fact their worry was not that they would be attacked or cheated if they made human contacts, but that they would be *infected* – a far more sinister probability. Yet the effect was the same: they were isolated and lonely, and, in the words of Jessie, the gardener's daughter, who loved them, 'they lived in fear all their lives'.

Eleven

THE BOOK ON MUNTJAC was the last that Eileen published. She was only sixty-four when it came out, and she had plenty of energy left for writing, painting and drawing; but circumstances conspired to dissipate her creative effort, and gradually, over the next twenty years, the sheer grind of life wore her down.

The worst single blow was the attack of spinal arthritis that had laid Eva low in 1967. For some time she had suffered from arthritis in her hands, but now suddenly she was hardly able to walk, and quite unable to garden or do household chores. This meant that Eileen's main domestic and horticultural support was cut from under her: instead of having meals prepared, and some basic gardening done, so that she was free to work in the studio, she now had to do all the cooking, and what gardening she could, and also to look after Eva.

Her letters began to show increasing signs of strain. 'We would love to come to Taunton,' she told Ernest Neal in September 1970. 'I am always longing to get to the West Country, but Eva has now become very badly crippled by arthritis, and cannot journey anywhere. She finds walking very difficult and painful. I battle on trying to cope with house, garden and wildlife – a hopeless task, as the garden is out of hand. The only help we can get is from an old-age pensioner who is as slow as a snail.'

To Winwood Reade she wrote:

Getting into the car is a very painful process [for Eva], which makes her hesitate to go out at all. Gardening is impossible for her, and we have only a pensioner who comes two mornings a week and crawls around. He is the slowest form of animal we have ever met! I just don't know which way to turn for the work in house and garden, and get very little time in the studio. We are constantly thinking of a move to a smaller and easier-run house, with many acres of field and a very small garden, but I simply do not know where to begin. With Eva crippled, I don't see how I could organise it all, to say nothing of clearing the junk here.

The problem was later compounded in 1975 by the fact that Eva had to undergo an abdominal operation, which left her dependent on the daily ministrations of a nurse. Yet she proved astonishingly durable, and lived on, mainly confined to her bedroom upstairs in the cold, grey house, for another fifteen years, creating untold work and worry for Eileen, but also furnishing her with a cast-iron excuse for repelling would-be visitors, refusing invitations and falling behind with her correspondence.

In spite of all her difficulties, Eileen kept up her work; and at the end of 1973 an attractive commission came her way when a former naval officer, Captain William Malins, wrote from Sussex to ask if she would illustrate his story about an orphaned female badger cub that had been reared by a bull terrier. She responded enthusiastically, and her drawings delighted the author. In due course *Bully and the Badger* was published, with some success; but unfortunately its life in the bookshops was cut short by the collapse of the firm that brought it out.

Eileen also maintained her contacts with other naturalists such as Ernest Neal, Garth Christian and Howard Lancum, and remained active in her efforts to win more effective protection for birds and animals. In September 1974, for instance, she wrote to John Adcock, producer of the BBC Television children's programme 'Blue Peter', asking him 'to consider putting out a plea to children and adults to refrain from taking large quantities of wild nuts and fruits and berries from the countryside in autumn', as 'the wild harvest forms a large part of the available food source of birds and mammals, including badgers, squirrels, deer etc.' She was often in touch with Peter Conder, Director of the Royal Society for the Protection of Birds, sometimes seeking advice on avian problems, and sometimes asking for the Society's help in defending her own sanctuary against the threat of development all round. When the RSPB launched an appeal for money to acquire new reserves, she contributed a picture which she valued at £35. On a different scale altogether, she began to make inquiries as to whether or not the RSPB would accept Wildings and its garden as a nature reserve, if she left the property to the Society in her will.

Throughout the 1970s she continued to draw and paint and send pictures to exhibitions, principally the annual show of the Society of Wildlife Artists, held in London, at which she generally had five or six watercolours hung; and she established a good relationship with the Wildlife Artists' Gallery which opened at Bourton-on-the-Water, in Gloucestershire, in 1972, selling several pictures through that channel. At about this date she acquired an important new friend in the form of Robert Gillmor, the leading bird painter, one of the founders (and later President) of the Society of Wildlife Artists. He had corresponded with her intermittently over the past five years, but now – a man exceptionally generous with his time – he began to give help in getting her pictures framed; when she

found it impossible to travel, he became a vital link with the art world, and she came to trust him as she trusted few others. When he married, in the autumn of 1974, she gave him a picture of fox cubs as a wedding present; and when, that October, he sent her a card from his honeymoon address in Argyllshire, she wrote that the picture of kittiwakes – from one of his own paintings – took her 'back to the cliffs and the seabirds' cries'.

She also went on writing, though less prolifically than before, and for years wrestled with a book provisionally entitled *An Artist Looks at Wildlife* – a 'guide to finding, watching and sketching animals in their natural habitats'. This compendium of advice contained much good sense, and firmly reiterated the author's most basic principle:

Accurate drawing is the fundamental feature of all true art, and vital in the representation of natural history, though many people who practise so-called 'modern art' appear to think

Opposite:
Muntjac in bamboo thicket

that drawing is unnecessary. The portrayal of beauty has become unfashionable among a section of the art world, but nature's superb example is always inspiring to the sincere artist, and combined with good technique gives true value to creative work.

Yet the book as a whole was dry and dull. One trouble was that it went over ground which the author had often covered before; another was that Eileen withdrew herself from the text: instead of including the precise, first-hand accounts of her own experiences that had so enlivened her earlier natural history books, she now wrote in generalities and from a distance. 'Permission to watch should be obtained from the landowner ... Shrews are common in the countryside ... Clothes for watching must be carefully chosen.' The text suffered further from the fact that its aim was imprecise: was it meant for children or for adults? Eileen never resolved that question, and even after many drafts the book remained unpublished.

Another project with which she struggled for years was the book of her father's engravings and etchings. Her original idea, conceived in the 1960s, had been a volume of straightforward reproductions; but during the 1980s this evolved into an anthology of country writing interspersed with illustrations, and she devoted an enormous amount of effort to planning such a work. Into two large folios she pasted typewritten extracts of poetry and prose, with copies of George Soper's prints between; and, with characteristic disregard of the messy background, she made a second version in superannuated issues of the *Radio Times*, sticking her typed excerpts over the old programme timetables.

In a preface she went straight back to a scene from her own childhood:

Winter had passed almost overnight, and the clear atmosphere had suddenly brought to life the hidden colour – the scents and sounds that define the first moments of spring, with its strange mingling of joy and sadness that is never more than half explained. Across the sunlit sky clouds were flying before a fresh wind that lifted the wings of the crying plover and gull, and on the wide expanse of field a man was ploughing, driving his team, splendid in colour and movement, seeming then as

durable as the land and its purpose, a sight inspiring to the artist's eye.

We stood on the high bank watching the horses as they passed rhythmically to and fro over the hill to the skyline, and down the long slope of the furrow to turn at the headland beside us. My father was sketching – he was never without his sketchbook on such occasions – and as he worked, the spontaneous, flowing lines of his pencil captured the life and movement of his subject with a freshness and vigour that reference to his work, whether in pencil, colour or engraving, brings intimate recollection of innumerable incidents and scenes depicting the life of the countryside, so much of which I shared with him, and which will never be seen again in Britain.

For the main part of the book she brought out all her old favourites – W. H. Hudson, Andrew Young, Edward Thomas, George Ewart Evans, H. J. Massingham, John Stewart Collis, Henry Williamson, H. M. Tomlinson, and, more often than any other, Vita Sackville-West, whose turgid, book-length poem 'The Land' she held in excessive veneration. Among the extracts from these other authors, she included several poems and prose-pieces of her own, some taken from her earlier books, some unpublished – and once again, with unusual vigour and feeling, she articulated her concept of the artist's role. In spring, she wrote,

The familiar landscape has a rare brilliance, broad and simple in its wider aspect, yet in detail as momentous, for one cannot turn without coming on some small miracle of sunlight – some renewal of colour hidden through winter: lichen on the barn roof and on the trees tangled in shadow; the sullen pond awake with colour from the sky; the rick, warm in reflected light; beauty of withered grass, of stones, the hidden buds of coltsfoot opening to the sun.

All these, and a thousand other subtleties of light and tone, the artist sees with a perception that goes far beyond the mere awareness of spring. The tide of inspiration sweeps him forward in his attempt to recreate the indefinable mood and quality of nature that challenges him on every side. In this, if he succeeds, is his joy, in failure, grief. But even this cannot deflect him from his purpose, and serves merely to impel new effort. He cannot turn back, for if ambition dies in the artist, the very meaning of life dies with it.

Altogether, Eileen's assembly of material was rich and diverse, and, enhanced by her father's prints, it would have made an anthology ripe with nostalgia for the far country of her childhood. But somehow she could never complete it to her satisfaction, and for years it remained unfinished.

Her own artistic ambition flickered on, and in 1979, in spite of injuries to her right hand and arm caused by a fall in the garden, she managed to complete the illustrations for Phil Drabble's book *No Badgers in My Wood*. But in her last years her talent was all but smothered by the weight of domestic chores and by her own increasing infirmity – for she too became bent with arthritis, and resented her physical weakness. 'The garden is ruined,' she wrote to a friend in 1980, 'and all our lovely plants are destroyed.' She scarcely exaggerated, for nature, left on its own, had stealthily undone the good work begun by her father seventy years earlier. Weeds and grass took over the iris beds. The roses went unpruned. Saplings sprouted from the lower lawn, where once the girls had played tennis. Elsewhere, trees and shrubs grew unthinned and unrestrained until they blotted out the light beneath them, killing all ground-plants except ivy. The sanctuary, which had once offered warm cover to deer and birds, became so gaunt and hollow that the wind whistled through it. All this distressed Eileen greatly; but the chaos inside the house worried her less, for it built up so slowly that it became part of the fabric of her life, and seemed perfectly normal.

Her own health was faltering. 'Last year I was found to have anaemia,' she told her friend the artist Ralph Thompson early in 1984. 'With this and rheumatism, gastric trouble, trigeminal neuralgia etc. I have not been feeling very cheerful ... Everything seems to be falling apart ... The garden is a complete wilderness, with nine-foot high nettles through spring and summer. The birds and beasties love it, but plants are gnawed to the ground by mice, voles, rabbits, deer etc. It is all heartbreaking from the gardening point of view.' Yet there was one substantial compensation:

Badgers are coming to feed on the terrace close to our windows. I saw them during last year's drought, when three and a young fox came to feed early in the evenings. Now there is only one, and he does not often come early, but when I can't sleep I sometimes get up and find him feeding in the early hours of the morning . . . I had known they were visiting the garden for a number of years, having seen their spoor and the remains of bees' and wasps' nests they had dug out. But I never hoped to see them. For me it seems like a little miracle.

Even Eva could look down from her bedroom window through a gap in the top of the pergola and watch the badgers as they trundled up for their supper under the spotlight. Both sisters still also watched birds with the keenest enthusiasm, and various feeding ledges and boxes fastened to the outside of the house brought them to close quarters.

Gradually the old ladies came to rely more and more on their neighbours Malcolm and Hilda Holt, who lived in Cherrybell Cottage, the next house up Harmer Lane, only fifty yards from Wildings. The Holts had been viewed with grave suspicion when they arrived in 1958, not least because they had a cat, and then wanted to build a garage next to Eileen's; but over the years they established themselves as indispensable friends and helpers, performing countless services and acts of kindness. Malcolm would act as chauffeur on Eileen's increasingly rare trips to London, drive her pictures up for framing, fetch apples for the deer in autumn, cut the grass, mend domestic appliances, ferry captured mice to distant release-points, fasten nesting-boxes to strategically sited trees, especially outside the studio window, and generally make himself useful. When Eva was stricken by arthritis, he made a sedan chair, so that she could be carried round the garden. Hilda would do the shopping, and, increasingly, the cooking. She found that Eileen was always meticulous about money: never mean, but extremely careful. When presented with an itemised bill, she would check it minutely before paying it, for she hated to waste a penny. One curiosity for the Holts was that, from their lawn, they could look straight into the studio window, and there, staring out at them almost as if it were a living being, stood the portrait of Eric Liddell, still on the easel.

Another good friend of Eileen's last years was Michael Clark, a naturalist, author and artist very much after her own heart, who

lived a five-minute car trip away at Tewin. Wildlife was the link that brought them together: in the 1960s Clark had been appointed county mammal recorder for Hertfordshire, and so became much involved with badgers and deer. Indeed, he tried to act as a go-between when Eileen fell out with Oliver Dansie; and, after that row had died down, from time to time she would telephone, asking him to come over and discuss the latest badger problem. At Wildings he did once manage to peep into the old kiln room, but otherwise he penetrated no further than the little parlour beside the kitchen. There she would receive him, painfully uncurling her bent back into a little seat beside the telephone, and they would chat for perhaps half an hour at a time. In winter the house always seemed freezing, and Clark would urge her – in vain – to turn the heating up (she did, by then, have electric night-store heaters). In spite of frequent requests, she refused absolutely to let him photograph her. 'Come on,' he would say. 'You're one of the great Hertfordshire naturalists. You really should be on record' – but she would never allow him to take a picture. Although he and his wife Anna repeatedly invited her to drop in at their house, she never did. 'If I'm passing,' she would say, but usually she would invoke Eva as her excuse for not coming.

She was, he found, a great wheedler, skilful at manipulating people and getting them to do things for her. Thus, even though he had a full-time job as a teacher, and, later, ten acres of his own to keep in order, he would sometimes be persuaded to come down with a scythe or chain-saw and make an attempt to tidy up the nearer reaches of the garden. But to him, as to all the part-time assistants whom she summoned, she could be perfectly infuriating, for she would always stop them doing what was obviously needed. As a man went to cut back the wisteria, she would cry, 'No, no! Not that much!' – and in the end most of them went away in disgust.

One visitor who called during Eileen's old age was Alison Boardman, formerly Earle, who as a child had several times sat to be drawn and painted in the studio. Now, seeing the artist after a long gap, Alison was distressed to find how much she had changed: not only was the house chaotic but Eileen herself was unwelcoming and querulous, complaining that although she was ill her doctor would do nothing for her (in fact she was so self-opinionated in medical matters that she never took a doctor's advice unless it

coincided with her own preconceived ideas).

Wildings itself had almost seized up. Not only were the rooms crammed with bric-à-brac: the hot water system functioned so poorly that it took at least an hour to run a bath. Yet when a local plumber, Ken Brunt, tried to sort out the pipes, he was stymied by Eileen's absolute refusal to grant him access to one locked cupboard. What was in it, he never knew, but without being able to work inside it he could not cure the problem, and he too went away frustrated. Anyone who attempted to call at the house unannounced was liable to be sent packing by a shout from an upstairs window. Eileen still sometimes went out in her car, and not until 1987, when she was eighty-two, did she give up driving, proud of the fact that she had kept her licence clean for sixty-five years. At last, however, she faced up to the fact that she was too infirm to be on the road, and sold her car to the Holts.

Throughout the winter of 1988–9, Hilda Holt cooked the old ladies' lunch and took it across to them. Aged though they might be, they had not grown one whit less demanding, and meals had to be prepared to their precise specifications. On every day of the winter, their menu was exactly the same: fillets of sole, poached in

139

milk and then browned under the grill, with breadcrumbs and a knob of butter on the top; potatoes steamed in their jackets, and peas, also steamed. For pudding they would have Symington's table creams, vanilla flavoured, made from the contents of a packet mixed with boiled milk and set in a mould. With them they would have some cooked fruit, usually Cox's Orange Pippins – for, like the muntjac, they would eat no other apples. As Hilda later remarked, she made table creams until she had them coming out of her ears.

When Eileen at last fell seriously ill, in March 1989, she was taken into hospital, then to a nursing home. She was not – it must be said – by any means a model patient. Cantankerous and demanding, she incited Michael and Anna Clark to smuggle in the numerous medicaments she kept at home rather than accept what the nurses offered her. Penetrating the upper fastnesses of Wildings for the first time, they were amazed to find a whole arsenal of drugs ranged on shelves beside her bed – but of course they could not give them to the patient, for fear that they might have clashed dangerously with medicines she was receiving anyway.

Eileen's burning desire was to return home, and her solicitor Graham Field did everything in his power to help her achieve her aim. He was faced, however, by formidable obstacles. Everyone concerned – not least health authorities and nursing associations – agreed that the old ladies could not possibly return to the house in its present state. If they went at all, they would have to have day and night nurses living in, and before any nurse would consider the job the whole place would have to be cleared out and comprehensively modernised.

Field handled Eileen brilliantly, with exactly the right mixture of tact and firmness (and a bit of teasing thrown in), and somehow he persuaded her to have the work done. By her standards, the expenditure was colossal – about £25,000; but she knew perfectly well that she and Eva could afford it, and she saw that unless the refurbishment was carried out she would never return home. So, in the summer of 1989, workmen moved in to install new plumbing, new bathrooms upstairs and down, a new kitchen, an electric chair-lift on the stairs and many other improvements. Before they could start, however, some at least of the rooms had to be cleared, and such was the accumulation of possessions that this proved no easy task: the kiln-room, for instance, was so packed that all Robert Gillmor and his wife Sue could do at first was to stand inside the door and start enlarging the space around them. At least the mystery of the 3000 empty glass jars was solved. Eileen had kept them not in case she suddenly wanted to make vast quantities of jam, but as a conservation measure. For years the local council had tipped household waste into an old chalk-pit, and she had been afraid that if she threw the jars out, they might smash in the pit and cut the feet of any badger that came to dig there.

She was beset by another anxiety as well: that she must somehow arrange publication of the anthology of country pieces, illustrated by her father's wood engravings, on which she had worked so long. She had taken the dummy copies of it into hospital with her, and she plagued people who visited her there or in the nursing home with demands for help. It was Robert Gillmor who managed to work out a compromise that brought her much relief: in London he arranged for publication not of the anthology, but of a book of the watercolours by George Soper which he had unearthed in the studio at Wildings. The mere fact that he had taken her typescript in hand, and that something positive was being done about a book, gave Eileen immense pleasure and encouragement: the knowledge that full colour would be used delighted her more than she could say.

In the autumn of 1989, work on the house proceeded apace, and one evening a plumber was startled when he heard a scratching noise at the door, and, on opening it, found a badger that had come in search of its supper. Eileen herself took a keen if quixotic interest in the way things were going. 'As long as they don't change anything,' she kept saying, knowing full well that fundamental innovations were being made. 'As long as they don't ruin the garden.' Yet she remained direly worried by the thought that strange men were at large in the house, and she exacted from Field a promise that nobody would open the locked cupboards in which she and Eva had kept their underwear.

Michael Clark, meanwhile, had been charged with the task of catching and removing the yellow-necked mice at large in the building, and one evening, as he drove home with two captives in a transparent polythene bag, preparing to release them in his own orchard, there took place an extraordinary incident. He was holding the mice in his right hand, on the steering wheel, when suddenly a kestrel made a pass at them, hurtling in at them from his right, and only at the last instant banking hard to clear the car's roof.

The sisters never went home. Eileen was taken to visit the house one day, to see how the improvements were coming on, and she seemed pleased with the progress made, if a little bewildered. She particularly liked the close-carpeting, in her favourite shade of blue, which had been laid in all the main rooms. But in March 1990 she suddenly began to fail, and in less than a week she died, without having seen even a proof-copy of the book on which she had set her heart. Her will left everything, in the first instance, to her sister.

Eva, mercifully, never understood what had happened, and countered the news of Eileen's death with an unanswerable observation. 'Of *course* she hasn't died,' she said when someone tried to explain. 'If she had, she would have told me.' But then, to the amazement of the nursing home staff, she gradually emerged from the chrysalis in which her sister had kept her imprisoned for the past forty years. While Eileen was alive, neither of them had left the room they shared, on the grounds that it was too dangerous to mix with the other inmates of the home; but now, freed at last from domination, Eva came out and mingled happily with the rest. Declaring that she had never really been a vegetarian at heart she asked for a helping of chicken. When she saw the dust-jacket of the book, now entitled *George Soper's Horses*, it thrilled her, and clearly it stirred some ancient memory, for she claimed to remember the painting, of two horses ploughing, from which it was taken.

Yet her life also was coming to its end, and she died in September 1990, aged eighty-nine, leaving a quarter of a million pounds. In their joint wills the sisters left Wildings and its garden to the RSPB, in the hope that it would remain a bird sanctuary; all the family's art work went to the Artists' General Benevolent Institution, and the leading London dealer Chris Beetles undertook to organise the sale of pictures, to the charity's best advantage, over the next few years. Some clue to the value of the Soper inheritance emerged when the Wildlife Art Gallery at Lavenham, in Suffolk, staged an exhibition of George's watercolours and engravings during September 1990. People came from all over Britain – from

Cornwall and from Scotland – to see them, and every watercolour in the place was bought on the first morning of the show. Individual prices ranged almost up to £3000, and the sale raised over £100,000.

Eileen's long struggle was over. But the flame of the artist had burned in her to the very end. On 1 April 1989, in the last year of her life, she wrote to Robert Gillmor, thanking him for a bunch of primroses he had picked in his garden and taken to her in hospital. After a note of heartfelt gratitude, she ended with a poem, the most moving she ever wrote:

> You brought to me a posy sweet
> That I might feel again
> The mosses growing at my feet
> And touch the silvered rain.
> You brought it not in vain.
>
> Such woodland flowers I brushed to cheek
> When days were young and gay
> Yet now are long away.
>
> But are these flowers? Or a brush of gold
> That in my eager hand I hold?
> And can this flame once more set free
> A humble painter's ecstasy?

Eileen. A. Tokery.

A Portrait by Reginald Haines, 4, Southampton Row, W.C.